28.9
56.7

# THE DEVIL'S BONES

# THE DEVIL'S BONES

## JEFFERSON BASS

𝔴𝔪

WILLIAM MORROW

*An Imprint of HarperCollinsPublishers*

*To our families*

---

THE DEVIL'S BONES. Copyright © 2008 by Jefferson Bass, LLC. All rights reserved. Printed in the United States of America. No part of this book may be used or reproduced in any manner whatsoever without written permission except in the case of brief quotations embodied in critical articles and reviews. For information address HarperCollins Publishers, 10 East 53rd Street, New York, NY 10022.

HarperCollins books may be purchased for educational, business, or sales promotional use. For information please write: Special Markets Department, HarperCollins Publishers, 10 East 53rd Street, New York, NY 10022.

FIRST EDITION

*Designed by Lovedog Studio*

Library of Congress Cataloging-in-Publication Data has been applied for.

ISBN 978-0-06-075985-8

08 09 10 11 12 ov/rrd 10 9 8 7 6 5 4 3 2 1

# CHAPTER 1

THE LAST DROP OF DAYLIGHT WAS FADING FROM THE western sky—a draining that seemed more a suffocation than a sunset, a final faint gasp as the day died of heatstroke. To the east, a dull copper moon, just on the downhill side of full, struggled above the crest of the Great Smoky Mountains. From where I stood, in a ridgetop pasture above the confluence of the Holston and French Broad rivers—above the headwaters of the Tennessee—I had a ringside view of the demise of the day and the wavering birth of the night.

Just below the ridge, across the river on Dickinson Island, the lights of the Island Home Airport winked on, etching the runway's perimeter in white and the taxiway in cobalt blue. The main landmarks of downtown Knoxville shimmered a few miles farther downstream—two tall office towers, a wedge-shaped Mayan-looking Marriott, the high bridges spanning the river, and the looming waterfront complex of Baptist Hospital. A mile beyond those, as the fish swims, lay the University of Tennessee campus and Neyland Stadium, where the UT Volunteers packed in a hundred thousand football fans every game. Football season would kick off with a night game in three weeks, and the stadium's lights were ablaze tonight, in some sort of preseason scrimmage against the darkness. The lights loomed high above the field; a series of additions to the stadium—an upper deck and skyboxes—had taken the structure higher and higher into the sky; another expansion or two and Neyland Stadium would be the city's tallest skyscraper. The lights themselves were almost blinding, even at this distance, but the water softened their reflection to quicksilver, turning the Tennessee into a dazzling, incandescent version of Moon River. It was stunning, and I couldn't help thinking that even on an off-season night Neyland Stadium was still the tail that wagged Knoxville.

Tucked beneath the stadium, along a curving corridor that echoed its ellipse, was UT's Anthropology Department, which I'd spent twenty-five years building from a small undergraduate major to one of the world's leading Ph.D. programs. A quarter mile long and one room wide, Anthropology occupied the outer side of the stadium's dim, windowless second-floor hallway. Mercifully, the classrooms and labs and graduate-student offices did possess windows, though the view was a bizarre and grimy one, consisting mainly of girders and cross braces—the framework supporting those hundred thousand foot-stomping football fans in the bleachers, keeping them from crashing down amid the countless human bones shelved beneath them.

Many of the bones catalogued in the bowels of Neyland Stadium had arrived by way of the Anthropology Research Facility—

the Body Farm—a three-acre patch of wooded hillside behind UT Medical Center. At any given moment, a hundred human corpses were progressing from fresh body to bare bones there, helped along by legions of bacteria and bugs, plus the occasional marauding raccoon or possum or skunk. By studying the events and the timing as bodies decomposed under a multitude of experimental conditions—nude bodies, clothed bodies, buried bodies, submerged bodies, fat bodies, thin bodies, bodies in cars and in sheds and in rolls of scrap carpeting—my graduate students and colleagues and I had bootstrapped the Body Farm into the world's leading source of experimental data on both what happens to bodies after death and when it happens. Our body of research, so to speak, allowed us to pinpoint time since death with increasing precision. As a result, any time police—police anywhere—asked for help solving a real-world murder, we could check the weather data, assess the degree of decomposition, and give an accurate estimate of when the person had been killed.

Tonight would yield a bit more data to the scientific literature and a few hundred more bones to the collection. We were conducting this experiment miles from the Body Farm, but I had brought the Farm with me—two of its inhabitants anyhow—to this isolated pasture. I couldn't conduct tonight's research so close to downtown, the UT campus, and the hospital. I needed distance, darkness, and privacy for what I was about to do.

I turned my gaze from the city's glow and studied the two cars nestled in the high grass nearby. In the faint light, it was hard to tell they were rusted-out hulks. It was also difficult to discern that the two figures behind the steering wheels were corpses: wrecked bodies driving wrecked cars, on what was about to become a road trip to hell.

■   ■   ■

THE TOW-TRUCK driver who had brought the vehicles out to the UT Ag farm a few hours before—minus their cadaverous drivers—clearly thought I was crazy. "Most times," he'd said, "I'm hauling cars like this *to* the junkyard, not *from* the junkyard."

I smiled. "It's an agricultural experiment," I'd said. "We're transplanting wrecks to see if a new junkyard takes root."

"Oh, it'll take root all right," he said. "I guaran-damn-tee you. Word gets out there's a new dump here, you'll have you a bumper crop of cars and trucks and warshin' machines before you know it." He spit a ropy stream of tobacco juice, which rolled across the dirt at his feet and then quivered dustily for a moment. "Shit, I know all *kinds* of folks be glad to help with *that* experiment."

I laughed. "Thanks anyhow," I said. "Actually, I lied. We are doing an experiment, but it's not agricultural, it's forensic. We're going to cremate a couple of bodies in these cars and study the burned bones."

He eyed me suspiciously, as if I might be about to enlist him forcibly as one of the research subjects, but then his face broke into a leathery grin. "Aw, hell, you're that bone-detective guy, ain't you? Dr. Bodkin?"

"Brockton"— I smiled again—"but that's close enough."

"I knew you looked familiar. My wife's a big fan of all them forensic shows on TV. She talks about donating her body to you'uns. But I don't think I could hardly handle that."

"Well, no pressure," I said. "We can use all the bodies we can get, but we're getting plenty. Nearly a hundred and fifty a year now. We'll put her to good use if she winds up with us, but we'll be fine if she doesn't."

He eyed the bed of my pickup truck, which was covered by a fiberglass cover. "You got them bodies yonder in the back of your truck?"

I shook my head. "If I did," I said, "you'd see a huge swarm of flies around it. Hot as it is, you'd be smelling something, too. We'll wait till the last minute to bring them out here. And we'll use a UT truck, not mine."

He nodded approvingly—I might be crazy, I could see him thinking, but at least I wasn't dumb enough to stink up my own truck. After unloading the cars from the bed of the wrecker, he'd given me a big wave and a couple of toots of the horn as he drove away. If he told the tale well to his forensic-fan wife over dinner, I suspected, he might be able to persuade her to donate her body to *him* tonight.

"**I'M STILL** shocked we're replicating something that happened at the Latham farm." Miranda Lovelady, my research assistant of the past four years, edged up beside me in the twilight. "I've been in that barn a dozen times and been in the house two or three. I always liked Mary Latham. Hard to believe she died in a car fire."

"Apparently the D.A. has a hard time believing it, too," I said, "since he personally called both me and Art to look into it. You never told me how you knew the Lathams."

"It was during my brief career as a veterinary student," she said. "Mary was friends with some of the vet-school faculty, and she liked to throw parties out at the farm. I got on her guest list somehow. Or her husband's." Her voice took on a slight edge when she mentioned the husband—now the widower.

"You don't sound too fond of him," I said, hoping she'd elaborate. She did.

"I had to fight him off in a horse stall once," she said.

"Jesus," I said, "he tried to rape you?"

"No, nowhere near that bad," she said. "He made a pass at me, and he didn't want to take no for an answer." She fell silent, and I had the feeling there was more to the story than she was telling. "He was a jerk, but he wasn't dangerous. At least, I didn't think so. But maybe I was wrong."

"I might wish I hadn't asked," I said, "but what were you doing in a horse stall with him?"

Another pause. "It was a vet-school party," she said. "The animals were part of the guest list. And *no*," she said sharply, "I don't mean it *that* way. The beer keg was always in the barn. There'd be bowls of apple slices to feed the horses." Despite the darkness, I glimpsed a smile. "I still half-expect to smell hay and hear horses nickering whenever I smell beer." The smile faded. "It was a lot of fun. Until it wasn't." She shook her head, as if shaking off a bug or a bad memory.

"When's the last time you saw the Lathams?"

"Her, right after I switched to anthro; him, about a year later. I quit going to their parties, and he showed up at the bone lab one day. Said he wanted to make sure I knew I was always welcome at the farm. Anytime, he said." She nodded toward the cars. "We all set here?"

"I think so," I said. "Let me check with Art." I looked around and finally spotted Art Bohanan's dark form half hidden by the lone tree in the pasture. "Art!" I yelled. "Mind your manners—there's a lady present."

"Oh, sorry," he called back, stepping away from the tree and tugging up his zipper. "I thought it was just you and Miranda." He pointed at the tree. "I was just making sure this fine botanical specimen won't catch fire."

"Very eco-friendly of you, pig," said Miranda.

"That's 'Officer Pig' to you," said Art pleasantly. Like me, he'd long since learned to enjoy Miranda's sarcasm, since it was tempered by forensic smarts, a tireless work ethic, and a big heart. Besides, Art had an equally sizable streak of smart-ass himself. His East Tennessee roots had infused him with a down-home sense of fun. His three decades of crime-scene and crime-lab experience—he was the Knoxville Police Department's senior criminalist—had added a dark, gallows topspin to the hillbilly humor. Working with Art practically guaranteed a Leno-like monologue of deadpan jokes about murders, suicides, and extreme fingerprinting techniques. ("Give me a hand, Bill," he'd once said at a crime scene; he was asking me to amputate a murder victim's right hand so he could rush it to the lab for fingerprinting.) To someone unaccustomed to daily doses of death and brutality, our humor might have sounded shocking, but Art—like Miranda, and like me—took his work seriously. It was only himself and his colleagues he took lightly. It made the bleakness bearable.

"Okay," I said, "we've got both bodies in position, we've got an amputated leg in each backseat, we've poured two gallons of gasoline into both passenger compartments, we've hosed down the area till it's the only patch of mud within a hundred miles, and we've got the water truck standing by with another five hundred gallons just in case. Anything I've forgotten?"

"You've forgotten to explain why it is we had to wait till my bedtime to get started," said Art. "It's not like the night's all nice and cool for us. It's still ninety, easy, and if that moon burns off some of this haze, it could get back up to ninety-five here pretty soon."

"It's not the heat," I said to Miranda, "it's the stupidity. You want to explain it to Sherlock here?"

"Sure, boss," she said. "I live to serve." She turned to Art. "Our primary objective, of course, is to incinerate all the soft tissue, so we end up with nothing but burned bones—comparable to the ones in the case you're working."

"I understand that," said Art, "and I do appreciate it. No, really. But don't dem bones burn just as good in the daytime as they do in the dark? Or is there something you osteologist types know that we mere mortals are not privy to?"

"Many things, grasshopper," said Miranda. "The bodies and bones *burn* just as well in the daytime, but they don't *photograph* near as well, and we want to document the process in detail." She pointed to the four tripods and digital video cameras we'd set up beside the vehicles. One camera was aimed through each vehicle's windshield, another through each driver's window. "If we did this during the day, the video would show nothing but smoke. Lit from the outside, by the sun, the smoke steals the show. Lit from within, by the flame, the tissue shows up clear as a bell while it burns away."

"I knew that," said Art.

"I know you knew," said Miranda. "You were just checking to make sure *I* did. Right?"

"Right." Despite the slight grumbling about the late start, I knew that Art was glad to be out here, rather than bent over a computer screen swapping chat messages with pedophiles. Six months earlier he'd been given the unenviable assignment of creating the Internet Crimes Against Children Task Force, dedicated to ferreting out sexual predators who trolled the Web for young victims. Since then he'd spent countless hours posing as "Tiffany," a fourteen-year-old girl who loved to chat online. Although Art took pride in catching and arresting the sort of men who preyed on the Tiffanys of this world, he found the work sad, stressful, and dispiriting. So getting permission to work even one old-fashioned murder case—something he found wholesome by comparison to pedophilia—was a welcome break for him.

"Okay, you two," I said, "a little less conversation, a little more incineration."

Miranda fished around in a pocket of her jumpsuit. "Rock and roll," she said. She flicked a disposable lighter, and a jet of flame appeared at the tip. She swayed like a drunk or a stoner, waving the lighter, and sang, *"SMOKE on the WA-ter, a FIE-uhr IN the sky-y."*

I laughed. "Aren't you a little young to know that song, missy? That's from back in my heyday."

"My grandpa used to play it on the Victrola," she said, "whenever he grilled up a woolly mammoth he'd clubbed." She grinned, and her teeth shone golden in the glow of the flame.

"Very funny," I said. "Remind me to laugh on the way back to the old folks' home."

"Ouch," she said, but she wasn't smarting from my snappy retort. She took her thumb off the trigger, and the flame died.

"Serves you right," I said. "Okay, let's get some data." I walked toward one of the cars, and Miranda headed to the other. Fishing a book of paper matches from one pocket, I lit one—it took three tries to get enough friction from the tiny strip at the base of the book—then used that match to set off the rest. The matchbook erupted in a fusillade of flame, flaring bigger than I'd expected, and I reflexively flung it through the open window of the car. The gas-soaked upholstery ignited with a flash and a whoosh, and I wondered if I'd been too liberal with the accelerant. I also wondered, as I felt the heat searing my face, if I had any eyebrows left.

Through the rush and crackle of the growing fire, I caught the drone of an airplane overhead. A small plane, just off the runway from the nearby airport, banked in our direction. As it circled, the flash of its wingtip strobes illuminated the smoke from the burning cars in bursts, like flash grenades, minus the boom. I tried to wave them off, but if they could even see me, they ignored my frantic gestures.

Backing away from my vehicle, I glanced over at the other car, also engulfed in flames. Despite the intensity of the inferno, Miranda stood barely ten feet from the car, one arm shielding her face, a look of utter fascination in her eyes. I forced my way through the blast of heat and took her by the arm. "You're too close," I shouted over the hiss and roar of the fire.

"But look!" she shouted back, never moving her eyes, pointing into the vehicle at the figure slumped in the driver's seat. I looked just in time to see the skin of the forehead peel slowly backward, almost like an old-fashioned bathing cap. As it continued to peel backward, I realized that what I was seeing was a scalping. A scalping done by fire, not by knife.

"Very interesting!" I yelled. "But you're still too close. That's what we've got the video cameras for. This is dangerous."

As if to underscore my point, a thunderous boom shook the air. Miranda yelped, and I instinctively wrapped both arms around her and tucked my head. I saw a puff of smoke from one of the tires—the heat had increased the pressure and weakened the rubber to the bursting point. Miranda and I scurried to join Art in the shelter of the water truck. "I hope you took off the gas tanks," Art shouted, "or filled them up with water!"

"Why?"

"In case there's any gas left. You don't want any vapors," he said.

"Since they came from the junkyard—" I began, but I didn't get to finish the sentence. Just then the gas tank of the car Miranda had been standing beside exploded, and pellets of hot glass rained down on us like some infernal version of hailstones. The car's spare tire—launched from the trunk by the blast—arced toward the water truck, slammed into the hood, and smashed through the windshield. *It's going to be a long, hot summer, Bill Brockton,* I said to myself, *and you've got some serious 'splainin' to do.*

The circling airplane beat a hasty retreat into the safety of darkness, and a moment later I heard sirens.

# CHAPTER 2

MY PHONE RANG FOR WHAT SEEMED THE EIGHTY-SEVENTH time of the morning, and I was hardening my heart to the plea of the ringer—resisting the reflex to answer—when I noticed that the caller was my secretary, Peggy.

It wasn't as if Peggy could just roll back from her desk and lean her head through my doorway. My office—my working office, as opposed to my administrative, ceremonial office—was a couple hundred yards from hers, clear on the other side of the stadium. Years ago I had laid claim to the last office at the end of the long, curving hallway that ran beneath the grandstands. I was as far off the beaten track as it was possible to get, at least within the shabby quarters inhabited by the Anthropology Department. The isolation allowed me to get five times as much work done as I would if my desk were situated along the daily path of every undergraduate, grad student, and faculty member in the department. But the deal I'd made with Peggy, when I latched on to this distant sanctuary, was that any time she called, I'd answer. I could ignore the rest of the world, but not her.

"Hey," I said. "What's up?"

"Incoming," was all she said.

I was just about to ask for clarification when I heard a sharp rap on my doorframe. "Gee, thanks for the warning," I said. I hung up just as Amanda Whiting strode in, all pinstripes and power pumps.

"Do you have any idea how many local, state, and federal ordinances you violated last night with your little bonfire of the vanities?"

Amanda was UT's general counsel, and she took both her job and herself quite seriously.

"From the way you phrase the question," I said, "I suspect that 'zero' is not the answer you're looking for."

"It's the answer I wish I had," she said, "but it's not the answer I've got."

"Okay, I give up," I said. "How many?"

"I don't even know yet," she said. "For one, you didn't have a burn permit—hell, Bill, there's been a moratorium on open burning for the past month because everything's dry as tinder. For another, you destroyed state property."

"What state property—the circle of grass we burned?"

"The Ag farm's water truck."

Ooh. I had hoped she didn't know about the truck. "Come on, Amanda," I said. "I've seen university presidents throw out thousands of dollars' worth of perfectly good carpeting just because the office hadn't been redecorated lately. You're busting my chops about breaking the windshield and denting the hood of a twenty-year-old farm truck?"

She glared. "And the Federal Aviation Administration says you're a menace to air traffic."

I couldn't help it; I laughed. "That's like saying the candle is a menace to the moth," I said. "That plane went out of its way to come down and circle those burning cars. If anybody's a menace, it's that idiot of a pilot. Miranda and I could have been killed. Hacked to bits by the propeller. Aren't pilots supposed to keep at least five feet away from innocent bystanders and enormous fires?"

"You think this is all a joke," she said, "but it's not. What if the truck had caught fire? What if the house on the adjoining property had burned down? What if the plane had crashed or your graduate student had been hit by that wheel? Any of those things could have happened if something had gone just a little more wrong. And then the university would be held accountable. And I'd be the one who had to clean up behind you."

"But none of them did happen, Amanda," I said gently, trying to soothe her now.

"But they could have."

I was tempted to reply, *But they didn't,* only I didn't see much to be gained by it. Amanda and I could contradict each other all day long, like two bickering dogs, but we wouldn't have anything to show for it except sore throats and ragged nerves. "Can I show you something, Amanda?" She eyed me suspiciously, as if I were about to unfasten my pants and flash her, then acquiesced with a shrug. Twisting around to the table behind my desk, I picked up a left femur—a thighbone, burned to a grayish white—and held it under the lamp on my desk. "This is from one of the bodies we burned last night," I said. "You see these fractures? This rectangular, rectilinear pattern?" I pointed with the tip of a pencil, and she leaned in, curiosity gradually outweighing her indignation. "This body was partially skeletonized when we put it in the car, and the bone was already drying. Now look at this one." I took another femur from a second tray of bones and held it alongside the first. "This was green bone," I said, "from a fresh body. Lots of moisture still in the bones—just like green wood with lots of sap in it. See the difference in the fractures?" She gave it a perfunctory glance, but then her gaze sharpened and took hold of something, and her eyes darted from one bone to the other.

"The fractures in the green bone aren't as regular," she said. "They're more random." She peered closer. "They kind of spiral or corkscrew around the shaft, don't they? Almost like the bone is splintering apart instead of just cracking."

"Very good," I said. I debated whether to play her the video clip showing the scalp peeling off the skull but decided that might be too graphic. "You'd have made a good forensic anthropologist."

Her guard went back up—she guessed I was herding her somewhere that she didn't want to go. "So why are you showing me this? What's your point?"

"This difference in the fracture pattern of dry bone and green bone could be important in a murder case," I said. "Actually, not 'could be'—*is* important in a murder case. That's why I needed to do the experiment. The difference tells us whether the victim was burned alive or whether she'd been dead awhile." She frowned. "The police and the district attorney are trying to decide, right now, whether to charge someone with murder in this case." I was pushing my luck, but I decided to press a point. "Tell me the truth, Amanda," I said. "If I'd come to you and described this experiment—setting fire to two cars at night, with bodies and amputated limbs in them—how long would it have taken to get the approvals you'd need? Weeks? Months? Forever?"

She shrugged and held out her hands, palms up, unable or unwilling to guess.

"Let me ask you something else," I said. "You've been here, what, five or six years now?"

"Seven," she said.

"The Body Farm was already a fixture here when you came. If it hadn't been—if I came to you today and said, 'Listen, I think we need to set aside a piece of land where we put dead bodies and study what happens to them as they decay,' what would you say?"

"Frankly, I'd say you were nuts," she snapped. And then something shifted in her expression, and she laughed. "And I'm pretty sure I'd be right."

I laughed, too. "Maybe so," I said. "But the police and the FBI and the TBI don't think so. Or maybe they do, but they also appreciate the research we do. It helps them solve crimes. Isn't that worth a broken windshield or an FAA reprimand every now and then?"

She gave me a stern look, but it seemed at least partly for show. "Are you asking me for permission to break the rules? I can't give you that."

"No," I said. "Not permission. A little understanding. And maybe occasional forgiveness."

She took a deep breath and puffed it out between pursed lips. "I'm going to the beach next week for vacation," she said. "Would you promise to try—really, really hard—not to stir up any more trouble the rest of this week?"

I held up the first three fingers of my right hand, my pinkie folded down and tucked beneath the tip of my thumb. "Scout's honor," I said.

"Fair enough," she said, then hesitated. "There's one other thing," she said awkwardly.

"I've done something else wrong?"

"No," she said, "you haven't. Actually, I have. When Dr. Carter was killed . . ." I froze, and she faltered, possibly because of what she saw in my face when she mentioned Jess's murder. "I was too quick. . . . I didn't give you the benefit of the doubt," she said.

"You mean when you exiled me? Told me I wasn't allowed on campus?" I hadn't meant to sound bitter, but I did. Jess was a smart and capable medical examiner; she was also a lovely and spirited woman, and I was just beginning to fall in love with her when she was killed. Her death had devastated me, being suspected of her murder had stunned me, and being treated as a pariah by the university had just about knocked the last prop out from under me.

She reddened. "Yes," she said. "That's what I mean. We should have stood by you. *I* should have stood by you. I was wrong, and I apologize. It might be too little, too late, but it's all I can do at this point. Even attorneys sometimes need—what was it you said?—understanding and occasional forgiveness. But I was harsh when you were on the ropes, I know, and forgiveness might be too much to ask." She glanced down at her sleek black pumps, then turned to go.

"Amanda?" She stopped in the doorway and looked back at me. "I understand why you suspended me. I didn't like it—still

don't—but I do understand it. Now I'll try to work on the forgiveness part. " I stepped toward her and held out my hand.

She shook it and said, "Thank you." And then she was gone,
leaving only the brisk echo of her heels in the hallway. That and
the ghost of Jess Carter in my office.

# CHAPTER 3

THREE HOURS AFTER MY EXCHANGE WITH UT'S TOP legal eagle, a hawkish young prosecutor—Constance Creed was her name—looked up from a yellow notepad, adjusted her glasses, and took a step toward the witness box where I sat. "Isn't it true, Dr. Brockton, that there had been conflict between yourself and Dr. Hamilton for quite some time?"

"I'm not sure I would characterize it as conflict," I said.

"How would you characterize it, then?"

"I disagreed with the conclusions of one of his autopsy reports," I said. She waited, seeming to expect me to say something more, so I did. "And I expressed those disagreements."

She closed the distance between us and leaned forward, her face no more than two feet from mine. I shifted in the straight-backed chair and wished I could not smell the onions she'd eaten at lunch. She wore Coke-bottle glasses, the lenses round and a quarter inch thick at the edges; instead of magnifying her eyes, the concave lenses made them appear small and beady. "You 'expressed' those disagreements?" She removed the glasses and glared at me. As nearsighted as she must be, I knew that the gesture was purely for effect, and I wondered how blurry my features appeared to her. I briefly considered making a face at her, to see if she'd even notice, but decided that the outcome of the experiment could get unpleasant if she did notice. Creed's eyes were an icy blue, and even without the distortion of the lenses her pupils were barely the size of buckshot. "Wouldn't it be more accurate, sir, to say you destroyed Dr. Hamilton's reputation as a medical examiner?"

"No, I don't think—"

"Did you or did you not testify against Dr. Hamilton in the case of Billy Ray Ledbetter?"

"No, I didn't testify against Dr. Hamilton."

"No? I have a copy of the hearing transcript, and it quotes you at length. Was that another forensic anthropologist named Dr. William Brockton?"

"No, that was me testifying," I said, resisting the urge to mirror her sarcasm. "But I wasn't testifying against Dr. Hamilton; I was describing an experiment. I tried to reproduce what Dr. Hamilton had described as a stab wound that killed Billy Ray Ledbetter. It wasn't possible to reproduce it—a rigid knife blade couldn't make the wound he described." As I spoke, I used one hand to demonstrate the zigs and zags that Hamilton's theory would have required. "My testimony disproved Dr. Hamilton's theory, but I wasn't attacking him. I was just reporting my research results."

"Just 'reporting your research results,'" she said sarcastically. "And were you also just 'reporting your research results' when you told the state board of medical examiners that Dr. Hamilton's conclusions 'violated the laws of physics and metallurgy'? Would you call that objective, scientific reporting?"

"I probably wouldn't use that phrase in a peer-reviewed journal article, but the fact remains—"

"The fact I'm interested in," she interrupted, "is who initiated the contact between you and the board of medical examiners—the board or you?"

I felt myself redden. "I think maybe I did."

"You think? *Maybe?* Do you consider it a trivial matter to call a physician's competence into question? A matter not even worth remembering?"

"No, I—"

"I'll ask you once more, then. Who initiated the contact, the board or you?"

"I did."

"So you could 'report your research results' to them, too? Are all anthropologists so eager to report their research results?"

Something in me snapped then. "Damn it," I said, "Dr. Hamilton nearly sent a man to prison for a murder the guy didn't commit. A murder no one committed, because it wasn't a murder. That—*that*—is not a trivial matter, Ms. Creed. And I am not the one on trial for killing Jess Carter."

She leveled a finger at me, almost as if she were aiming a gun. "But you nearly were, weren't you, Doctor?"

"Okay, stop right there," I said.

"You were the prime suspect, weren't you, Doctor? In fact, initially *you* were charged with killing her, weren't you?"

"I said stop!"

"How did it feel, Doctor, to get off the hook for the murder and be able to point the finger at Dr. Hamilton?"

"Enough!" I shouted, leaping to my feet. "I loved Jess Carter, and I will not . . . How dare you . . ." My voice failed me, and I put a hand over my eyes.

I felt a hand on my shoulder, warm and steady. "I'm sorry, Dr. Brockton," I heard her say, suddenly sounding human and pained. "I hate to put you through the wringer. But believe me, this is gentle compared to what Hamilton's attorney will do next week during the trial. When he gets up to cross-examine you, he will go for your throat like an attack dog. You're our key witness, so the defense will do everything they can to undermine you, throw you off balance, make you mad."

I looked up, and she met my gaze steadily, compassionately. Her eyes didn't look beady now; they just looked tired, from years spent straining to see the world through a wall of glass and the darkness of crime. "God, this is hard," I said. I fished out my handkerchief, wiped my face, and blew my nose.

"I know," she said, "and I wish I could tell you it'll get easier. But it won't."

*Great*, I thought, *nothing like an encouraging word.*

"Think of this as a scrimmage, or maybe war games, so you're mentally prepared for the real thing. You were doing great till right there at the end. It's okay to get sad on the stand. Just don't get mad. If you get mad, you're playing their game. They'll make you look vindictive, and they'll make him look like a victim."

"But there's a recording of him admitting he killed Jess. A recording of him *bragging* about killing Jess."

"They'll try to suppress that. Or undermine it any way they can. Besides, it's a recording, and a pretty scratchy one to boot. Your testimony will carry a lot more weight with the jurors than that. So roll with the punches and hang on to your temper, for God's sake. For Dr. Carter's sake."

We sparred a few more rounds, the prosecutor and I. Finally, after two hours of rolling with the punches of her mock cross-examination, I was allowed to step down from the witness stand she'd set up in the practice courtroom. I left the City-County Building and headed along Neyland Drive feeling jangled and un-settled. It wasn't until I found myself taking the Cherokee Trail exit off Alcoa Highway that I realized I wasn't heading back to my office but to the Body Farm. Even after I realized that, it took a moment longer to grasp *why* I was headed there.

There were no other cars in the distant corner of the hospital employees' parking lot that bordered the research facility. The chain-link gate was locked, as was the high wooden gate within. Even so, after letting myself in, I called out to make sure I had the place to myself. When I was certain of that, I locked the gate behind me and walked up the hill into the woods.

It was the first time I'd had the nerve to visit the spot in the three months since I'd dug the recess in the rocky dirt and laid the slab at the base of the big pine. The black granite was dull with dust, so I knelt down and took a handkerchief to it. The grime proved more stubborn than I expected, so I wiped my face and neck with the cloth to moisten it—one pass got it plenty damp—then set to work on the marker again. "Sorry about the sweat, Jess," I said. "You never were the squeamish sort, so I'm thinking you wouldn't mind."

The moisture loosened the dirt, and after I'd turned and folded the handkerchief several times to expose clean fabric to scrub with, the black granite gleamed again, silver flecks of mica shimmering within its depths. Closing my eyes, I ran my fingers across the surface. The chiseled edges of the inscription tugged at my fingertips and clutched at my heart. In Memory of Dr. Jess Carter, Who Worked for Justice, the words read. Work is love made visible. I laid my palm on the warm stone, flat and steady, the same way Constance Creed had laid hers on my shoulder not long before. I thought back to the period when Jess and I had been mere colleagues—she a rising star among the state's medical examiners, me an odd-duck anthropologist who conferred with corpses as they turned to goo or bare bones. It seemed several lifetimes ago, though in fact we had collaborated platonically scarcely six months before. Then I flashed ahead to the night everything had changed.

"God, Jess, I miss you," I said. We had spent just one night together, but that night seemed to encapsulate years' worth of meaning. And it had cost Jess her life. Garland Hamilton had followed me to Jess's house, had lurked outside, listening, as we made love, and then—just days later—had abducted Jess from a restaurant parking lot, taken her to his basement, and shot her. In a final, perverse twist, he'd staged her body in a gruesome tableau here at the Body Farm—here at this very tree—and had nearly succeeded in framing me for the murder.

It haunted me to realize that, given a chance, Jess and I might have built a remarkable life together, a rare partnership of like minds and kindred spirits. "I guess we'll never know," I said aloud, but even as I spoke the words, I knew they were false: I did know, all the way down to my core. Only three things in my life had ever rung true enough to redefine everything else. The first was the life I'd built with Kathleen, my late wife, and our son,

Jeff. The second was the bizarre career path I had half followed, half created. The third, I was realizing only in hindsight, was the love I'd begun to feel for Jess.

Kathleen and I had shared a solid, steady love, and it carried us through three decades of partnership and parenthood, until cancer claimed her three years earlier. I'd spent two years grieving for Kathleen. Then, to my surprise, I was ready for love again; ready for Jess.

Back when I was in college, I'd taken a class in Greek mythology, and we'd read Homer's *Odyssey*. Since Jess, an image from Homer kept coming back to me: the marriage bed of Ulysses and Penelope. Ulysses had carved their bed from a mammoth tree trunk, still rooted in the earth, and then built their home around it. It was a secret known only to them—the secret by which she would recognize him when he returned from his years of warfare and wandering. The love Jess and I were starting to discover could have been like that, I sometimes thought—something rooted in earth and bedrock, a mystery understood only by us—if we'd had the chance to build around it. If Garland Hamilton hadn't uprooted it, driven by jealousy of Jess and hatred of me.

Hamilton had been enraged to learn that Jess was about to become the state's chief M.E. But he had murdered her not just out of a misplaced sense of rivalry. He'd done it mainly to hurt me—to break my heart before killing me as well. The second part of his plan had failed, and Hamilton was now facing a possible death sentence for killing Jess. But Jess's death was a wound I'd carry far longer than if he'd killed me. Yet I'd also be carrying the memory of Jess, and though I'd always mourn the loss, I'd never regret the love.

"I miss you, Jess," I said. "And I'm so sorry."

The only answer was the dull thud of helicopter rotors as a LifeStar air ambulance skimmed low above the Body Farm, inbound to UT Hospital with a patient hanging between life and death.

# CHAPTER 4

AFTER MY VISIT TO JESS'S MARKER, I WASN'T READY to face my empty house. I called Jeff, my son, and asked if I could swing by for a visit.

"Sure," he said. "We're just about to grill some burgers. Come on out—I'll throw one on for you."

"Hmm, charbroiled meat," I said, picturing my recent nighttime experiment. "I'm not sure I'm all that hungry."

"Have you seen a doctor yet? You must be ill. I've never known you to turn down anything cooked on the grill."

"Long story," I said. I realized that my need for company outweighed my aversion to the smell of searing flesh. "I'll tell you over dinner."

Jeff's house was about fifteen miles west of downtown Knoxville, in the bedroom community of Farragut. Compared to Knoxville's other bedroom communities, Farragut tended toward bedsheets with a higher thread count. Named for a Civil War hero born nearby, Admiral David ("Damn the torpedoes") Farragut, the town was a sprawling collection of upscale shopping centers, golf courses, and subdivisions with names like Andover Place and Berkeley Park. There was no downtown; the "town center" consisted of a municipal building that housed a library branch and a county clerk's office. Across the parking lot was a post office, a bank branch, and a couple of restaurants. Farragut wasn't my idea of a town, but it seemed to suit a lot of people, because it was the fastest-growing part of Knox County.

Jeff and his wife, Jenny, and their two boys, Tyler and Walker, lived at the end of a quiet cul-de-sac, the sort of place where parents still let their kids roller-skate and ride bikes in the street. Maybe that was the appeal. Maybe in some ways Farragut was a town, or pieces of a town, the way towns used to be, back before the streets became places of peril.

I saw a wisp of smoke curling up from behind their house, so I let myself in the wooden gate to the backyard and circled around to the patio. Jeff was just spreading out a glowing mound of charcoal briquettes. His hands were smudged with soot, and his face glistened with sweat.

"Glad to see you haven't gone over to the dark side and switched to gas," I said.

"Never happen," he said. "You taught me well, and I've eaten too many tasteless burgers at my neighbors' houses."

"You know, of course, it's the carcinogens that give the good smoky flavor," I said.

"Actually," he said, "not necessarily. Apparently some researchers at Johns Hopkins did a study on this very thing. The carcinogens form when you let the fire flare up—for some reason that particular temperature causes a chemical reaction that creates the carcinogens. So you don't want to cook the meat over open flame—just hot coals. Close the lid, hold in the smoke, keep the fire low, and everything's okay."

"I'll sleep better knowing this, son."

Jenny came out the back door with a platter of burgers. "Hey, Bill," she said. I liked it that she called me "Bill" rather than "Dad" or some other in-law title; it allowed us to relate as equals. "Good to see you."

"Good to see you, too," I said. I noticed their boys peering out the glass of the storm door. Tyler was seven, and Walker was five. Both were wearing the baseball uniforms they seemed to live in all summer long.

Jenny followed my gaze. "Guys, come on out and see Grandpa Bill," she called, a little too cheerily.

They did as they were told, but they hesitated, and that hesitation nearly broke my heart. It had scared and confused them when I was charged with Jess Carter's murder. Their friends had said cruel things to them, as children will do, about Grandpa the killer. A parent can do a lot of explaining, but it might still take years to restore the openness and easy trust my grandsons had once felt with me. By then, of course, they wouldn't be five and seven anymore.

Jenny set the burgers down on the patio table and came up to give me a hug and a kiss on the cheek. The warm greeting was partly for my sake, but partly for the boys as well—a message to them that yes, I was still their grandfather, and yes, I was someone safe to love.

Jenny looked searchingly into my eyes, and this part, I knew, was just for the grown-ups. "How are you?" she said.

"I'm okay," I said. "Mostly."

"I think about you all the time," she said. "I'd give anything if I could undo all the things that went wrong last spring."

"Me, too," I said. "Sometimes I feel lonelier than I did before Jess—or maybe I just notice the loneliness more now. The trial starts next week, and I figure that'll be hard. But maybe once it's done, I'll feel some closure. I want to hear sentence pronounced on him. And I want it to be a harsh one."

"Would you like us to be there when you testify?"

I didn't trust my voice to answer the question, so I just nodded.

"Then we will," she said. "You tell us when, and we'll be there. And if there's anything else you need, you call Jeff or you call me."

I nodded again.

"Promise?"

"Promise."

# CHAPTER 5

"Dr. Brockton? This is Lynette Wilkins, at the Regional Forensic Center."

Lynette didn't need to tell me who she was or where she worked; I'd heard her voice a thousand times or more—every time I dialed the morgue or popped in for a visit. The Regional Forensic Center and the Knox County Medical Examiner's Office shared space in the morgue of UT Medical Center, located across the river and downstream from the stadium. There was also a custom-designed processing room—complete with steam-jacketed kettles and industrial-grade garbage disposals—where my graduate students and I could remove the last traces of tissue from skeletons after they'd been picked relatively clean by the bugs at the Body Farm. From fresh, warm gunshot victims to sun-bleached bones, the basement complex in the hospital dealt with them all.

"Good morning, Lynette," I said. "And how are you?"

"Fine, thank you."

"Glad to hear it," I said, although she didn't actually *sound* fine. She sounded extremely nervous and formal—an odd combination, I thought, in a woman who had once, at a Christmas party, planted a memorable kiss on my mouth. Spiked punch could be blamed for most of that lapse in office decorum; still, our frequent conversations—in person and by phone—had been marked by the ease and casualness of comrades-in-arms, fellow soldiers in the trenches of gruesome accidents and grisly murders.

"Dr. Garcia, the medical examiner, would like to speak with you," she said, and as I pictured an unfamiliar M.E. sitting a few feet away from her, I understood why she didn't sound like her usual self. "Could you hold on for just a moment?"

"Sure, Lynette," I said. "Have a nice day."

The line clicked, and I waited. Nothing. I waited some more. Still nothing. Then I heard a man's voice say, "Ms. Wilkins, are you sure he's there?" A pause followed, then, "I don't think so."

"Hello," I said.

Another pause.

"Mr. Brockton?"

Now it was my turn to pause. "This is Bill Brockton," I said. "Dr. Bill Brockton. How can I help you?"

"This is *Dr.* Edelberto Garcia," said a cool voice, whose careful emphasis was meant to let me know that not all doctors are created equal. His first name sounded elegant and aristocratic the way he pronounced it—"ay-del-BARE-toe"—but then I remembered a bit about Spanish pronunciations, and I realized that the English version of his name would be "Ethelbert," and I nearly laughed. "I've been appointed by the commissioner of health to serve as director of the Regional Forensic Center."

"Sure," I said, resisting the urge to add "Ethelbert" to my answer. "I had lunch with Jerry last week. He told me he'd hired you. Welcome to Knoxville."

"Thank you," he said. If he noticed my first-name reference to Gerald Freeman, the health commissioner, he didn't let on. I considered adding that six weeks earlier Jerry had shown me the files on the three finalists for the job, and had asked for my opinion. Garcia had been my second choice—and Jerry's, too—but the strongest of the finalists had taken a job at a far higher salary in the M.E.'s office in New York City.

"We're currently investigating the death of a Knoxville woman whose burned body was found last week in her car," he said. Again I nearly laughed out loud.

"Why, yes," I said, "I believe I heard something about that. Can I be of some assistance?"

"I'm told by a police investigator, a Sergeant Evers, that you've done some—shall we say *research*?—that might be relevant."

"Ah, Sergeant Evers," I said. "Good man, Evers. Dogged investigator. Fearsome interrogator." I didn't add that Evers had fearsomely interrogated *me* only a few months before and had arrested me on suspicion of homicide, in the death of Jess Carter, who had served a brief stint as acting M.E. here in Knoxville. Maybe Garcia already knew that; if he didn't, he was the only person in a hundred-mile radius who didn't. "If Sergeant Evers thinks my research might be relevant, far be it from me to disagree." I could hear him weighing my words and my tone for the sarcasm I'd added to them, and I suspected he was about to respond by turning even more stuffy and condescending. No point getting into a pissing match with the new M.E., I decided. "Actually, Dr. Garcia, that research *is* pretty interesting. What we've done is compare fire-induced fractures in green bone—fleshed bone—with fractures in dry bone. We burned two cars containing cadavers and limbs from the immediate postmortem interval, as well as from one week and two weeks postmortem. No point going past two weeks in the summer—by then you're down to bare, dry bone already."

He mulled this over briefly. "And have you documented your research results? Do you have something you could messenger over?"

"Nothing in writing," I said. "Got some burned bones I could messenger over."

"Thank you, but without some methodological context, I'm not sure—"

"Hell, I'll be the messenger, and I'll give you the context," I said. "I'm coming over that direction anyhow. I'll bring a few of the bones and show you what it is I'll be writing up, soon as I get around to it. You can ask questions, and I can try to answer them. If any of it's relevant, great. If it's not, neither one of us has lost more than a few minutes. You want to take a look?"

"Very well," he said.

*Very well?* I thought. *Who says "Very well" anymore? And why does this guy have such a big broomstick up his ass?* "Swell," I said, then thought, *Who the hell says "Swell" anymore, Brockton?* Then I thought, *Apparently I do.* "I'll be over there in about ten minutes. Looking forward to meeting you."

"I'll see you then," was all he said before hanging up.

I selected half a dozen bones from the fiery nighttime experiment, then wrapped them in bubble wrap and laid them in one of the long boxes we used to store the specimens in the skeletal collection. As I headed down the hall that traced the curve of the stadium's end zone, I passed the open door of Jorge Jimenez, a Ph.D. candidate in cultural anthropology from Buenos Aires. Jorge's name sounded anything *but* aristocratic, I realized, since the first syllable was pronounced like "whore." I tapped on Jorge's door with one knuckle. "Come in," he said, not looking up from his computer screen. The screen showed a young couple doing what appeared to be the tango, but suddenly they spun apart and began break-dancing.

"That's an interesting dance," I said. "I don't believe I know that one."

"Ah, Dr. Brockton," he said, looking up. "Sorry to be rude. This is actually research. Did you know that in Buenos Aires, where this dance video was shot, one out of every twenty teenagers has posted a video on YouTube?"

"I didn't," I said. "What's U-2?" It didn't sound like he was talking about a Cold War spy plane or a rock band.

"Not U-2. YouTube." He scrawled it on a piece of paper for me. "An Internet site where people post videos they've made. Very popular with young people. Like MySpace."

"Your space? You have a Web site that's popular with kids?"

He laughed, then typed an address into his computer's browser and called up a page filled with flashing ads and thumbnail pictures of faces and pets. "Not *my* space," he said. "MySpace .com."

After a few seconds, he clicked it back to the tango break dancing. "At first all the videos on YouTube were very clumsy and silly," he said, "but a lot of them these days look like something straight out of Hollywood." He studied my expression again. "But I think you didn't stop to talk about cinema or the Internet."

"No, I stopped for advice," I said. "Do you have any tips on dealing with a Latino physician who seems to have a chip on his shoulder?"

"You mean Eddie Garcia?"

Eddie? I smiled. It was better than Ethelbert. Or Ethel. "How'd you know?"

"Lucky guess." He smiled back. "What you need to remember is that he's not just Hispanic, Dr. B., he's Mexican, so you might need to cut him some slack."

"What does *that* mean?" I asked. "If you weren't Hispanic yourself, I'd think that was more than a little patronizing."

"If I were a gringo, it *would* be patronizing. But I'm Latino, so it's not." Confusion was written all over my face, and he speed-read it and smiled. "All Latinos may be created equal," he said, "but we're not all treated equally, even by one another. East Tennessee has Latinos from just about every country in Central and South America, and some of them look down on the Mexicans as harshly as any Tennessee redneck or Georgia cracker ever did."

"How come?"

"Part of it's just snobbery—there are so many Mexicans in the States that they're not exotic, the way Venezuelans or Chileans are. It's like a lawn or a garden—if one strange plant bursts into bloom, it's a wildflower; if a bunch of them spring up, they're considered weeds."

"Not by the other plants," I pointed out.

"True," he conceded, "so the analogy's not perfect. But you get the point?"

I nodded.

"Then there's the pecking order of the workplace. Mexicans often take the shit jobs. They mow yards and lay brick and wash dishes and change linens—anything to get their foot in the door—while people like me get visas to study engineering or anthropology or medicine. So the white-collar Latinos look down on the blue-collar Latinos, and the Mexicans are mostly blue-collar."

"But Garcia's not," I pointed out. "He's a board-certified M.D., a forensic pathologist."

"But that's recent. He's been Mexican all his life. And his parents were working class, so he knows what it's like to be looked down on. He comes by that chip on his shoulder honestly."

"I wouldn't have thought of that," I said. "So you know Garcia?"

"A little. Eddie's okay. Yeah, he's a little touchy. But cut him some slack, talk some shop, and things should be fine. He's a forensic guy, you're a forensic guy. Bond over the bones, Dr. B."

"Jorge" I said over my shoulder, "you could have had a brilliant career in psychology. You're pretty damn smart, for a Latino."

He laughed. *"Bastardo!"* he called after me. I decided that was Spanish for "Amen, brother!"

GARCIA STOOD and nodded slightly when I entered his office at the Forensic Center, but he didn't offer a hand, so I simply returned the nod. "Please, have a seat," he said.

"It might be a little easier if we laid these bones out on a lab table," I said.

"Very well," he said again. *Swell,* I thought. *Mr. Personality.* I followed him down the hallway to the main lab and set my box on a countertop. The counter was covered with a large, absorbent blue pad, which helped cushion the fragile bones. I had brought three femora—femurs; thighbones—which I laid side by side. Garcia leaned down toward the closest, which was from the body that had been fully fleshed when it burned. The bone exhibited a range of colors, from ashy white at the distal end, near the knee, to a deep reddish brown at the proximal end, where it had joined the hip.

I chose my words carefully, as I didn't want to appear to be lecturing him, even though I was. "We used two gallons of gasoline in each car, so it was a very hot fire," I said. "It peaked at around two thousand degrees Fahrenheit—about eleven hundred Celsius. It burned away all the soft tissue, except for some on the central region of the torso." I pointed to the femur from the fresh cadaver. "Down here at the distal end, the bone is obviously completely calcined, since the lower legs and knees get more oxygen and burn away before the thighs and torso do. Up here, where the thicker muscle tissue provided some protection for a while, the bone started to char, but it's not calcined."

He studied the bone closely.

"There's still some organic material in there," I went on. "You could probably get DNA—at least mitochondrial DNA, if not nuclear DNA—from a cross section of the bone up in this region."

He nodded.

"What's really interesting to me," I went on, "is the fracture pattern here. It's very irregular. Notice how the fractures seem to corkscrew around the bone in a sort of helical pattern. There's also some fracturing between layers of the bone."

"Yes, very interesting," he said, sounding more animated. He reached up and swung a magnifying lamp into position, switching on the light that encircled the back side of the round lens. "It's almost as if the bone is peeling apart. From the moisture inside turning to steam?"

"Probably," I said. "Now compare that to the dry, defleshed bone. It's completely calcined, not surprisingly, since there was no muscle to shield it. Notice how regular and rectangular the fracture pattern is, almost like cross-hatching."

He repositioned the magnifying glass over the uniformly burned femur.

"This reminds me of a big log," I said, "that's been burned very slowly in a bonfire."

"Or a dead tree lying in the desert," he said. "After years in the sun, they get that same burned look."

"Here's another one for you," I said. "I was over in Memphis a few summers ago, when they had the worst drought in a century. The Mississippi River dropped fifteen or twenty feet. It exposed huge sandbars, a half mile wide and miles long. Walking on them was like walking along the beach at the ocean. And the river shrank from a mile wide to a narrow channel, a few hundred yards across—I could have skipped a rock to the other side."

His mouth twitched, but I wasn't sure if he was suppressing a smile or stifling a yawn. Either way, I was caught up in the memory.

"It was the most remarkable thing," I said. "The sand was golden and clean—not what I'd expected, since the river is as murky as day-old coffee. Right beside the channel, the sand sloped down like this." I angled my hand at forty-five degrees. "If you took a running jump, you'd go flying over the edge, drop ten feet or so, then sink halfway to your knees near the bottom of the embankment." I had leapt off that slope of sand a dozen times that day, and a hundred more since, in my memory. "There was a beautiful woman sunbathing, topless, in the middle of this vast expanse of sand," I said. "But what really caught my eye were the tree trunks, four or five feet in diameter"—I made an arc with my arms, wide as I could stretch them—"down on a narrow shelf, right at the edge of the river channel. They had that same charred look, and it fascinated me, how being underwater for a hundred years made those trees look burned."

He laughed, a soft, musical laugh from deep in his chest, and it was the first sound I'd heard him make that wasn't tightly reined in. "Are you always doing research, even when a beautiful woman is stretched out on the sand?"

"Pretty much," I said sheepishly. But I could see the absurdity of it, and I laughed along with him.

Garcia's face got serious again, but his gaze and his voice stayed open. "Would you like to see this burn case?" he asked. "No, wait, that's not exactly what I want to ask you. Would you please take a look at this burn case, Dr. Brockton? I would be very interested in your opinion."

"Very well," I said with a smile and a slight bow. "I would be honored, Dr. Garcia."

He motioned me into the main autopsy suite, then disappeared into the morgue's cooler and emerged a moment later wheeling a stainless-steel autopsy table. As he folded back the drape, I felt my adrenaline spiking, the way it always did when I confronted a forensic puzzle. Garcia began talking, almost as if he were dictating notes. "The subject is a deceased white female, positively identified from dental records as Mary Louise Latham, age forty-seven." According to what I'd learned from Art and Miranda and the newspaper stories, Latham had lived in Knoxville all her life.

She and her husband, Stuart, lived on a farm along Middlebrook Pike, in northwest Knoxville. I was fairly sure I knew the property. Middlebrook Pike had been transformed in recent decades into a corridor of warehouses, petroleum tanks, and trucking depots; there was only one farm, as far as I knew, along Middlebrook, and the prettiness of it was underscored by its uniqueness. The land was a mix of rolling pastures and wooded ridges, with a graceful old farmhouse and a well-kept white barn. It wasn't really a working farm these days, more like a hobby farm, with a couple of milk cows, a handful of chickens, and a half-acre vegetable garden. The Lathams had no children, but Mrs. Latham often invited elementary-school groups to visit and learn about farming.

In less than an hour, a burning car had reduced her to charred remnants. Some of the small bones of the hands and feet were missing—probably fragmented and embedded in a layer of ash and debris in the car's floor pan. The blackened bones of the arms and the lower legs were devoid of soft tissue, even burned soft tissue; they were calcined at their distal ends but not at the proximal ends, where they'd joined the torso and had gotten less oxygen. The pelvis and torso still had tissue on them—if you could call the scorched, crusty material clinging to the bones "tissue." What had once been the cranial vault had been reduced to shards of bone, resembling small, burned bits of shell, none of them more than a couple inches across.

Garcia switched on the surgical light above the autopsy station and trained it on the bones. Then he offered me a pair of purple nitrile gloves, which I tugged on, as he did likewise with another pair. He touched a purple finger to the right leg, just below the knee. "This is interesting," he said. "Up here near the proximal end of the tibia, the fractures look like the ones you just showed me in green bone." Leaning in, I saw the spiraling, splintered pattern left behind after flesh has burned away, and I nodded in agreement. "But down here at the distal end"—he pointed—"the fractures are more regular." Sure enough, just above the ankle, the bone was neatly crosshatched with cracks.

"Huh," I said. "Looks almost like two different cases—one involving green bone, the other involving defleshed bone—rolled into one tibia." Studying the rest of the body, I noticed a similar trend in the other limbs.

"What do you make of that?"

I didn't answer. I wasn't ignoring him; I was just distracted. Something lodged in the skull—deep within a shattered eye orbit—had caught my attention. Reaching to the counter along the wall, I selected a pair of long tweezers and eased their tips down into the recess, trying to tease out the tiny object. "Do you know," I asked, "whether the car's windows were up or down?"

"Three of them were up, but the driver's window was down a few inches," he said. "There were several cigarette butts on the ground underneath it. Why do you ask?"

"I was wondering what sort of access the blowflies might have had to the body."

"All the car windows shattered in the fire. So the flies had plenty of access but not much time. When I arrived, the car was still too hot to touch. I don't remember seeing any flies."

"I don't mean after the fire. I mean before."

Garcia looked puzzled.

"Unless her brain was infested while she was still alive," I said, extricating the tweezers from the eye orbit, "the bugs had been working on her for days before that car burned." I held the tweezers over my left hand and deposited my prize in the palm. There on the drum-tight purple surface was an immature maggot, about the size and shape of a Rice Krispie. A Rice Krispie that had been thoroughly charred.

She hadn't been burned alive; she'd been burned dead. Dead and already decomposing.

# CHAPTER 6

I STARED AT THE CONTENTS OF THE PACKAGE AGAIN, then stared at the note once more. *"Dr. Brockton, please call me when you get this. Thanks. Burt."*

I dialed Burt DeVriess. I didn't have to refer to the number embossed on the fancy letterhead; I remembered it from the brief, memorable, and ruinously expensive period when DeVriess—better known as "Grease" throughout Knoxville's legal (and illegal) circles—had served as my criminal defense attorney. Grease had charged me an arm and a leg, but he had also saved my neck, so it was hard to begrudge him that fifty-thousand-dollar retainer. His secretary, Chloe, seemed to think that our association had saved some part of Grease as well, the part that passed for the attorney's shriveled soul. Judging by the years he'd spent ruthlessly representing Knoxville's seamiest criminals—his client list read like a who's who of killers, drug peddlers, and pedophiles—salvation seemed too much to hope for. Still, the fact was,

DeVriess had taken to turning down the notorious clientele that had made him rich and infamous. He'd not yet traded his Bentley for a Prius, as far as I knew, or started doing pro bono work for the homeless. But even if he hadn't attained sainthood yet, he at least seemed to qualify for some sort of "Most Improved Karma" award.

Chloe answered on the second ring. "Mr. DeVriess's office, may I help you?"

"Hi, Chloe, it's Bill Brockton."

"Hi there," she chirped. "How are you?"

"Hanging in there, Chloe. And you?"

"Pretty good, but we do miss you. You need to get yourself arrested again, so we'll see you more often."

"I can't afford it," I said, laughing. "If I had to hire Burt again, I'd go bankrupt."

"Perfect," she said. "Then he could represent you in bankruptcy court."

"For free, no doubt," I said. "So speaking of the master of legal larceny, what's the story on this package he sent me?"

"Oh, *that*," she said. "I think I'd better let him tell you about that. Hang on. And come see us?"

I smiled. Chloe had treated me exactly this way—as a friend—when I first walked in through her boss's art deco doorway with a murder charge hanging over my head, so desperate that I'd stooped to hire the aggressive defense lawyer I despised above all others.

While I held the line for DeVriess, I took another look at the contents of the package he'd sent me. It was a small wooden box, almost a cube, about eight inches square. It was ornately carved, with an engraved brass latch and a hinged top. The box was beautiful, but what really caught my eye was the grainy, powdery mixture I saw when I opened the lid.

"Hello, Doc," said a voice that managed to sound both butter smooth and granite hard at the same time. It sounded like money and power, and I knew that Knoxville's winningest defense attorney had plenty of both. "How's life down on the Farm these days?"

"People are dying to get in, Burt," I joked. "How's life down in the sewer?"

"Stagnating a little," he said cheerily. "There's a vicious rumor making the rounds that I've gone soft, maybe even developed a conscience. It's killing my practice, but it's great for my golf game."

"There's always a silver lining," I said. "As they say, if you can't have what you want, then want what you have. So this little present you sent me—is this what it looks like?" I stirred the upper layer of the mixture with the sharpened end of a pencil, and a tiny plume of dust rose from the box. Uppermost in the mixture was a layer of fine, grayish white powder; beneath that was a layer of grainy tan particles, along with what I quickly recognized as shards of incinerated bone. "I got excited when I opened the lid," I joked. "Thought for a minute maybe these were your ashes."

If he thought that was funny, he hid it well.

"So who is this, Burt?"

"That, Doc, is the sixty-four-million-dollar question," he said. "Supposed to be my Aunt Jean. But my Uncle Edgar? He says not."

"How come?"

"You looked at it yet?"

"Only a little."

"Notice anything funny?"

I stirred around a bit more, creating another miniature dust storm. Down near the bottom of the box, I glimpsed what appeared to be small, rounded pebbles. "Well, there's some rocks in here," I said, "As least they sure look like rocks."

"Damn right they look like rocks," he said. "Doesn't take a Ph.D. in anthropology to tell the difference between bone and pea gravel. Another thing? You wouldn't have any way of knowing this, of course, but Aunt Jean's knees aren't in there."

"Her knees? How do you know?"

"Because Aunt Jean's knees were made of titanium. She had both of 'em replaced about five years ago."

"Crematoriums don't usually send things like that back to the family, Burt."

"Uncle Edgar specifically asked for them."

"Ah. Then that would seem to be a significant omission."

"They couldn't have melted and dripped down somewhere in the oven or something, could they?"

"I don't think so," I said. "Those orthopedic devices are made of pretty tough stuff. But let me do a little research on titanium and cremation and get back to you."

"Could you do more than that, Doc?"

"What do you mean?"

"Something's not right here, Doc," he said. "What'd they do with her knees? What's that gravel doing in there? And how come those chunks of bone are so big? I scattered my mother's ashes up in the Smokies after she died, and there weren't any pieces bigger than rock salt in Mom's urn."

"So you want me to do a forensic analysis on this set of cremains?"

"Cremains?" He snorted. "Who the hell came up with 'cremains'?"

"Not me," I said. "Some funeral director, probably. Easier to say than 'cremated human remains,' I reckon."

"Cornier, too," he said. "Listen, I'll pay your hourly expert-witness rate, for however many hours you need to spend on this." My rate was two hundred dollars an hour; that meant I'd need to poke around in the cremains for 250 hours to recoup the fifty thousand dollars I'd forked over to Grease a few months earlier. I didn't want to spend 250 hours breathing the dust of Aunt Jean, but I was intrigued by the case—and impressed that the lawyer had zeroed in on the puzzling things in the mixture.

"I'll find out everything I can," I said.

"Thanks, Doc," he said. "I owe you."

"Not yet," I said, "but you will."

He laughed. "I guess I'd better sell one of the Bentleys," he said, but we both knew that my bill wouldn't amount to a fraction of what I'd paid Burt to defend me. He gave me a few more details—his aunt's date of death, the name of the funeral home and the crematorium, and the phone number of his Uncle Edgar, who lived in Polk County—then signed off, saying "'Preciate you, Doc."

I dialed the extension for the bone lab, tucked beneath the other end of the stadium, a five-minute walk through curving hallways along the base of the enormous ellipse. "Osteology lab, this is Miranda. Can I help you?"

"I sure hope so," I said.

"Oh, it's just you."

"Try to contain your enthusiasm," I said.

"Oh, ex-*cuse* me," she gushed. "Dr. *Brockton,* how may I be of assistance?"

"That's more like it," I said. "Soon as you finish genuflecting, could I trouble you to dig up the melting point of titanium?"

"I live to serve," she said. "Elemental or alloy?"

"I'm not sure."

I heard the rapid clatter of keystrokes. "Well, if you're talking pure titanium metal," she said, "the melting point is a toasty nineteen hundred and thirty-three. That's on the Kelvin scale, which is"—*clatterclatterCLATTERclatter*—"three thousand and change, Fahrenheit."

"How'd you find that so fast?"

"The wonders of Google," she said. "Google also lives to serve."

"Damn," I said. "Google, YouTube, MySpace—I feel like a dinosaur, Miranda."

"Well, admitting you have a problem is the first step toward change," she said. "So is that it? You just got curious about the properties of titanium?"

"No, actually, what I'm wondering about is the melting point of artificial knees."

I heard another flurry of keystrokes. "Looks like most orthopedic implants are made of titanium alloy, cobalt chromium steel, or stainless steel. Also oxidized zirconium—sort of a cross between a metal and ceramic—which is harder than metal but tougher than ceramic." More keystrokes. "The most common material seems to be titanium-662, though, an alloy of titanium, aluminum, and vanadium, plus a pinch of this and a dash of that."

"Vanadium? Is that really an element, or are you just making that up?"

"Making it up? *Moi?* You cut me to the quick. That would be a violation of the Research Slave Code of Ethics. Besides, if I were going to make up an element, don't you think I could come up with something better than 'vanadium'? I think 'mirandium' has a nice ring, don't you? And 'loveladium' rolls trippingly off the tongue, too."

"What was I thinking? You're right," I said. "The periodic table really should revolve around you."

"I'll let the implication that I'm egocentric pass for the moment, because I'm so delighted to be doing your grunt work. Let's see, titanium-662. . . . Melting point is . . . *durn* it . . . a closely guarded military secret, it would appear. Not really, but I'm not getting any Google hits that look like the answer. You want me to call some equally downtrodden peon in Engineering?"

"Nah, hold off for now," I said. "I wouldn't think the alloy's melting point would be a whole lot lower."

"You know what I think?"

"More often than I'd like," I said.

"Ha, ha. I think if you're running a high enough fever to melt your knees, you're long since toasted."

"Toasted is right," I said. "The question is, could a cremation furnace melt a pair of knee implants?"

"I'd say it depends how hot the furnace gets."

"Really? Amazing. Do the folks who give out the MacArthur genius grants know about you?"

"Don't get smart with me, boss."

"Or else?"

"Or else I'll hang up."

"*Ooh*," I said, "now you're *really* scaring me."

I laughed when the line went dead. I was pretty sure she was laughing, too.

My next call was to Norman Witherspoon, a Knoxville funeral

director who'd sent me a half dozen or so corpses during the past decade—people who'd wanted their bodies donated to science but who hadn't made the arrangements before dying. "Norm, what do you do when somebody asks to be cremated?"

"I say, 'Sorry, I have to wait until you're dead.'"

"Everybody's a comedian," I said. "Let me rephrase the question. Norm, where do you send bodies to be cremated?"

"East Tennessee Cremation Services," he said. "Out near the airport. In the Rockford industrial park, off Alcoa Highway."

"I've got a case involving cremated remains. You reckon East Tennessee Cremation would let me come look at their equipment and ask a few questions?"

"Long as the case doesn't involve them. Does it?"

"No," I said. "A place down in the northwest part of Georgia—Trinity Crematorium."

"Oh, *that* place."

"Why do you say 'that place'?"

"Well, that's where funeral homes send cremations if they want to save a few bucks or a little time."

"How many bucks is 'a few'?"

"Not too many—about a hundred per cremation. We handle about sixty cremation requests a year, so we'd save about six thousand dollars if we switched. But if you factor in Trinity's pickup and drop-off, the savings would be bigger."

"How so?"

"We have to take the bodies out to East Tennessee Cremation, and then we have to go pick them up, either at the end of the day or sometime the next day. So that's a hundred and twenty round-trips. We're only about fifteen miles from there, so it's not a huge problem, but it can get complicated, especially if we have several burials going on at the same time, too. Trinity picks up the bodies and then returns the cremains, and that can save a lot of time. They courted us pretty hard, and we thought about switching, but in the end we decided to stick with East Tennessee Cremation."

"Because?"

"I've known the folks there for twenty years. They do a good job, they keep their facility spotless, and they're extremely professional."

"Unlike the folks at that Georgia place?"

He laughed. "You sound like some fast-talking courtroom lawyer now. You've been spending way too much time being cross-examined. Look, I don't know anything bad about them. But I don't know anything great about them either. What it comes down to is, I don't want to stop doing business with people I know and like, just for the sake of a hundred bucks here and there."

"Fair enough," I said. "No further questions at this time. Oh, except the name and number of the person I should call at the place over in Alcoa?"

"EAST TENNESSEE CREMATION." The woman who answered sounded slightly out of breath, as if she'd had to dash for the phone.

"Is this Helen Taylor?"

"Yes. Can I help you?"

I introduced myself and began a convoluted explanation of why I was calling.

"Norm Witherspoon told me you'd probably be calling," she said, as soon as I gave her an opening. "I heard you lecture a few years ago at the Tennessee Association of Funeral Directors. You were showing pictures of how a body decays if the embalming job's not good. You're welcome to come out anytime."

I wasn't sure if she was extending the welcome in spite of my criticisms or because of them. Either way, I was quick to accept the invitation. "When would be a good time to visit?"

"Up to you. I'm here Monday through Friday, eight a.m. to five p.m. We've got three cremations scheduled today, so pretty much anytime you come, I'll be putting somebody in, taking 'em out, or running them through the processor."

"Sounds like they're getting their money's worth from you," I said. "No wonder you sounded winded when you answered the phone."

"There's not a lot of downtime, that's for sure," she said. "I'm just finishing one now, and I thought I'd start the next one right after lunch."

I checked my watch; I'd just eaten a sandwich at my desk, but I tended to eat early. It was not quite eleven-thirty.

"All right if I come on over in about an hour?"

"I'll be looking for you." She gave me directions, and after I'd gone through the morning's mail, I headed out. The mail gave me an idea, so on the way I made a quick stop by Peggy's. She wasn't in, luckily, because I was pretty sure she wouldn't have let me borrow her postage scale if she'd known what I planned to use it for.

# CHAPTER 7

FROM THE STADIUM I HEADED DOWNSTREAM ALONG
Neyland Drive, past the veterinary school and under the Alcoa
Highway bridge. The bridge pilings were marked with horizon-
tal lines at one-foot intervals, showing towboat pilots how much
clearance they had between the waterline and the bottom of the
bridge. *Why are they called towboats*, I wondered, *when they
move the barges by pushing, not pulling?* Between the heat and the
drought, the river was down as low as I'd ever seen it in summer.
That meant there was plenty of clearance overhead—fifty-seven
feet, according to the markings, which was two feet more than
usual. But two feet more clearance overhead also meant two feet
less water underneath. That wasn't a worry here, where the river
was narrow and the channel deep, but a few miles downstream
the river spread into broad shallows, where even a fishing boat
risked a mangled prop if it strayed from the center of the naviga-
tion channel. *We need rain,* I thought, *and a hell of a cold front.*

At the intersection of Neyland and Kingston Pike, I turned right, then also took the next right, onto the ramp for Alcoa Highway southbound. Crossing the high concrete bridge that I'd passed beneath only a moment before, I looked downriver, where the mansions of Sequoyah Hills lined the right-hand bank. I lived in Sequoyah, but my house—tucked into an incongruously modest little block of bungalows and ranchers—was probably worth one-tenth the price of these riverfront villas. I'd had the chance, when I first started teaching at UT, to buy one of the big houses, but the price—fifty-five thousand dollars—seemed astronomical at the time, at least on a professor's salary. Twenty years later that house was worth at least a million, maybe more. The ones lining the waterfront were even more expensive. "Yeah, but I don't have to worry about barge traffic washing away my yard," I said out loud, then laughed at myself. "Okay, Brockton, not only are you talking to yourself, but what you're saying is a total crock."

UT Hospital and the hills behind the Body Farm reared up on my left. On my right a UT cattle farm—green pastures dotted with black-and-white Holsteins—nestled in the big bend of the river. It was the place where the Tennessee first curved southward, starting its serpentine slide toward the Gulf of Mexico, sixteen hundred meandering miles away.

Acting on a sudden impulse, I veered off at the Cherokee Trail exit—the exit for the medical center—and threaded under the highway and around to the back corner of the hospital employees' parking lot. We'd received a donated body several weeks before, and I remembered a note in the chart indicating that the donor—a man in his seventies—had undergone double knee replacement within the past two years. That made his knees newer than any I'd dug out of the boxes in the skeletal collection, and I had a sudden hankering to see them.

I found him just off the main trail curving up into the woods and toward the river. He lay on his back near a fallen tree trunk, his skull detached and slightly downhill from his postcranial skeleton. A camera tripod stood nearby, with a black plastic mailbox fastened incongruously to the top. The mailbox was an improvised housing for a night-vision camera; the camera, sheltered by the weatherproof plastic, was connected to a motion sensor, so that when nocturnal carnivores—raccoons and opossums, mainly—came foraging, we could capture their feeding habits. The project was a Ph.D. candidate's dissertation research, and I'd marveled over some of the photos, which showed cuddly raccoons reaching deep into body cavities to pluck out special delicacies. In the cold, clear light of dawn—actually the scorching, hazy light of high noon—I could see gnaw marks on the cheekbones, the hands, and the feet. But I was more interested at the moment in the hingelike hardware installed where the knees had once been.

I'd had the opportunity during my teaching career to witness two orthopedic surgeries—a hip replacement and a cervical-spine fusion—and I'd come away from both procedures marveling at the combination of precise control and bloody brute force. The neck surgery in particular was an astonishingly choreographed performance by a neurosurgeon and an orthopedist. First they yanked and gouged out three crumbling disks from the patient's neck, at times reaming within a millimeter of the spinal cord; next they tapped pegs of precisely machined cadaver bone into place between the sagging vertebrae; finally they screwed an arched titanium bracket onto the front of the neck, to buttress the spine while the bones knitted together. As the pair of surgeons drilled and tapped and bolted, I couldn't help comparing them to cabinetmakers. The hip replacement by comparison was heavy carpentry—sawing off the proximal end of the femur, drilling a hole down into the shaft, and then pounding the stem of the metal prosthesis into the opening.

The body on the hillside—body 67–07, the sixty-seventh donated body of the year 2007—was almost entirely skeletonized after three weeks of decomposition. The metallic knees gleamed dully; faint saw marks were still visible where the arthritic joints had been cut away and removed from his legs. *Remarkable*, I thought, *that people can walk again after having their knees chopped out.* "Chopped" was probably not how this man's surgeon had described the procedure, but as I studied the trauma that had been dealt to the bones, the drastic verb seemed to fit.

My reverie was interrupted by the sound of a helicopter buzzing low over the treetops. The air ambulances of LifeStar often passed directly over the Body Farm on their way to and from the hospital's helipad, but this chopper, I realized, wasn't flying a typical approach. The pitch of the rotor blades seemed steep and urgent, and the aircraft wheeled and banked abruptly, repeatedly. A siren—then two, then more—screamed toward the hospital, and a second helicopter joined the cacophony.

Over the rising din I suddenly heard my name. "Dr. Brockton! Dr. B., where are you?" It was Miranda, and as she called me, I heard something I'd never expected to hear from Miranda Lovelady: I heard fear.

"Bill!" shouted a man's voice, and I saw Art Bohanan running toward me, Miranda two steps behind. Art's face was flushed, his eyes were as focused as lasers, and his weapon was drawn.

"What on earth?!"

Art said only a few words, but when I heard the fourth one, I felt my knees go weak.

"Garland Hamilton just escaped," he said.

# CHAPTER 8

ART GRABBED ONE OF MY ARMS AND MIRANDA grabbed the other, and they practically dragged me down the hill, through the clearing, and out the gate of the Body Farm. Miranda paused just long enough to close the gates and snap the padlocks shut, while Art led me to my truck, peering inside and even underneath before allowing me to get in.

Once Miranda was in her car, Art hustled into his unmarked sedan, hit the siren, and switched on the blue lights hidden inside the grille. With Miranda's Jetta in the rear, Art led us out of the hospital complex in a haze of smoking tires. As we careened onto Cherokee Trail, headed for Alcoa Highway, half a dozen police vehicles—KPD, Knox County Sheriff's Office, and Tennessee Highway Patrol—screamed past in the opposite direction.

Five minutes later Art, Miranda, and I surveyed one another glumly across my desk beneath Neyland Stadium. "How did this happen?" I said. "Where? When? With his trial coming up, I'd have thought Hamilton would be watched like a hawk."

Art sighed. "You and me both."

"Was he in the Knox County Detention Center? Hell, they've got cameras by the hundreds out there—I don't see how a prisoner could pick his nose without three cameras recording the boogers for posterity."

He shook his head. "The reason we hustled you away from the Farm so fast is that he was only a stone's throw away when he escaped." I stared at Art uncomprehendingly. "He was in the ER at UT Hospital. They'd rushed him there after he went into convulsions," Art said. "Or *appeared* to go into convulsions. As they were wheeling him into the ER, he jumped off the gurney and ran into a stairwell."

"Damn it," I said, "that's the worst possible place for him to get loose. He knows every nook and cranny of that hospital. If they didn't have it locked down in sixty seconds, he could have taken a hundred ways out."

"They didn't have it locked down in sixty seconds," Art said.

I didn't need him to tell me that. The chorus of helicopter rotors and police sirens told me Hamilton had gotten away. What I didn't know was where he'd go and what he'd do: lie low, slip away, or try again to kill me?

TWENTY-FOUR HOURS later, I was still in shock. I'd spent a bad night, followed by a dismal day and an even more wretched night. Every sudden noise made me jump, and the only thing worse than the sound of the phone ringing was the sound of it *not* ringing—the sound of Hamilton slipping silently away.

A security camera showed that Hamilton had ducked out through the back door of the Forensic Center only minutes after leaping off the gurney. In fact, he was already outside before the first KPD units were dispatched toward the hospital. Somewhere between the ER and the Forensic Center's exit, he'd tugged on a pair of scrubs and a surgical mask. One of the pathology residents later told police that he thought he'd glimpsed Hamilton in the hallway, but he'd dismissed the notion, since he knew—or *thought* he knew—that Hamilton was in custody.

Once beyond the loading-dock camera's field of view, Hamilton had vanished completely. It was possible he'd stowed away in the back of a linen truck or one of the dozens of other service vehicles entering and exiting the hospital complex daily. It was also possible he'd simply walked across a parking lot and slipped into the woods that bordered the grounds on the south and the east. Two days of searching—by tracking dogs, by helicopters, and by dozens of KPD officers, Knox County deputies, and TBI agents—had failed to turn up any leads.

Hamilton's escape was the lead story in the *Knoxville News Sentinel* and on every local TV station. His picture and Jess's and mine were prominently featured, and my house was once more besieged with reporters clamoring for sound bites describing how it felt to know that the man who'd killed Jess and tried to kill me was on the loose. The only consolation to the media frenzy was that if Hamilton showed up within a mile of my house, he'd be captured instantly, at least on videotape, by several news crews. The two days after his escape were among my life's lowest points—surpassed only by Kathleen's death, Jess's murder, and my arrest.

The third day I rose from the dead, or at least from the deadly paralysis of spirit that had gripped me. The only way to get my mind off Hamilton, I realized that day, was to get it on something else. One such something, I decided, could be unraveling Burt DeVriess's questions about his Aunt Jean's cremation.

I called Helen Taylor at East Tennessee Cremation and apologized for standing her up two days before. "If you're still willing to show me around, I'd appreciate it, but if you don't want to bother at this point, I understand."

She assured me she'd not taken offense—she'd seen me on the news after Hamilton escaped—and invited me to come out as soon as I could.

"Is thirty minutes too soon?" I asked.

"Thirty minutes is fine," she said.

I resumed the journey I'd begun two days before.

East Tennessee Cremation occupied a low, modest building on a grassy corner at the Rockford industrial park's entrance. Facing it, across the street, was a prefab metal warehouse identified as S and S Services. The crematorium was no bigger than a two-car garage and not much fancier, the owners apparently seeing no need to indulge in the frilly sentiment or veneered stateliness of funeral homes. I liked the unpretentious plainness—it was fitting, I decided, for a place that took in dead bodies, laid them in an incinerator of sorts, and burned them down to inorganic minerals. The building had a low L on one side, which housed an office with a glass door and double-hung windows. The business part of the building—the part in the higher, cinder-block portion—had a big roll-up garage door on the front end and two steel exhaust stacks on the other. The building had no sign of any kind; it was the stacks—their tops a swirl of bluish black that bespoke extreme heat—that told me I'd found the crematorium.

I knocked on the glass storm door, but I didn't get an answer, so I peered inside. The office looked vacant. The door was unlocked, so I stuck my head in and called, "Hello? Ms. Taylor?"

From around a corner, in the garage-looking part of the building, I heard a muffled female voice say, "I'll be right there."

A pleasant, fiftyish woman emerged. Dressed in a gray pantsuit and black pumps, she would have looked at home in a bank or real-estate office, except for the work gloves she wore—the leather-and-canvas kind favored by carpenters and farmers. She took off one glove and held out a hand.

"You must be Dr. Brockton," she said. "I'm Helen Taylor. Sorry to keep you waiting."

"I kept you waiting for two days," I said, "so you've still got a ways to go before you need to apologize. Thanks for agreeing to give me a look around." I shook her hand. She had a firm grip and an open, direct gaze that I liked. For some reason, maybe because so many funeral directors tended to look deferentially downward, I hadn't expected someone so forthright.

Helen had started out more than twenty years earlier working as a secretary in the office of a company that made metal cemetery vaults. Several years later, when the owner of the vault company branched out and opened a crematorium, he trained Helen to run it. After serving a two-year apprenticeship, she took the examination to become a licensed funeral director. Although she passed the exam with flying colors, the licensing board turned her down—they'd never licensed a female funeral director, nor anyone who'd apprenticed at an independent crematorium. After two years of training, Helen wasn't willing to take rejection lying down. She hired an attorney, who threatened to sue the licensing board for discrimination. A few weeks later, she received a letter containing her funeral director's license.

In its first year of operation, the crematorium had burned only four bodies, leaving her plenty of time for secretarial work. This year, she said, the number would top four hundred. Business was so good, in fact, that the crematorium was beginning an enormous expansion. She raised the blinds behind her desk and pointed out the window at a fresh excavation and enormous concrete slab. Within a year, she told me, they'd be moving to a new building five times this size. It would be equipped with a chapel for services, a viewing window, and a remote-control ignition switch, so a family member could push a button to start the cremation. The old building would remain a crematorium, but it would shift from cremating humans to cremating pets, a business that was growing by leaps and bounds. She pulled out a binder filled with architectural drawings and floor plans of the new building. I noticed it would have three furnaces rather than just two; I also noticed a large room labeled cooler, which I asked about. The cooler would be able to hold up to sixteen bodies, she told me proudly.

"Sixteen? That's a lot of bodies," I said. "Nearly as many as the Regional Forensic Center can hold. You're not planning to start killing people off, are you?"

She laughed. "I don't have to. I've had as many as six or seven bodies come through here in a day," she said. "Not often, but when it happens, I need someplace to put them. Can you imagine four or five bodies stacked up in here on a day like today?" She had a point there. The small building was air-conditioned, but between the blistering sun outside and the ovens inside, the temperature was probably close to ninety. She did need a cooler, and if business was growing like she said it was, it might not be long before she'd have that cooler filled. I was impressed with the operation, and when I said so, she beamed.

"If you'd told me twenty years ago this is what I'd be doing, I wouldn't have believed you," she said. "But here I am, and I love what I do."

"I'm sometimes surprised where I ended up, too," I said, "but I wouldn't change it. I'm never bored, I'm sometimes able to do a good deed for victims or families, and I get to meet interesting people like you."

"Let's go take a look," she said. She led me through a connecting door into the crematorium's work space, which was every bit as spartan and utilitarian as the outside had hinted it would be. This garage was a two-furnace garage, the ovens parked side by side, their stainless-steel fronts bristling with dials and knobs and lights. She pushed a button on the furnace on the left, and a thick door slid up, revealing an arched interior about eight feet long, two feet high, and three feet wide. The interior walls of the furnace were brick—a pale, soot-stained brick, similar to what I'd seen pottery kilns made of.

I edged up for a closer look. "You mind if I stick my head in?"

"Not at all," she said. "Just let me fasten this safety latch first—I'd hate for that door to fall and decapitate you." The door was six inches thick, its steel cladding insulated with a layer of firebrick; it probably weighed at least a hundred pounds. She fitted a stout, L-shaped cotter pin into a slot beneath the lower edge of the door, the guillotine's equivalent of the safety on a gun.

The firebrick—refractory brick, she called it—was tan and fine-grained, with several paler spots where small chips had flaked off. I reached up and rubbed a finger over one. A few grains, somewhere between sand and ceramic in texture, flaked off in my hands. "Does this just naturally flake away over time?"

She nodded. "They have to be relined about every two years."

The floor and the roof of the combustion chamber were made of concrete; a spiderweb of cracks zigzagged through the roof. "Are these cracks a problem? Can you just patch them, or do you have to chip out the whole top when you reline it?"

"Actually, those are normal," she said. "The very first time you fire up a brand-new cremation furnace, you get that cracking—the heat's so intense."

As I leaned in farther, an image from Hansel and Gretel popped into my head. "You're not going to shove me in," I said, "and turn me into gingerbread?"

"Not hardly." She laughed. "If I turn this burner on, you won't come out looking anything like a gingerbread man. Here, let me show you the 'before' version, and then I'll show you 'after.' It's quite a contrast." A metal gurney was parked along one wall of the building. It held a cardboard box the size and shape of a coffin. She tugged at the lid and raised it enough to give me a look.

An ancient man—not a day less than ninety, I guessed—lay within, slightly to one side of the centerline. He was thin and shriveled and had clearly been shriveling for years. There was room enough in the container for him and two more bodies his size. The man's face was collapsing into his mouth, and I knew without pulling down a lip that the jaws were toothless. The root sockets were probably long gone, smoothed out over the past ten or twenty years, as the bone resorbed and filled them in.

"Looks like he had a long life," I said.

"His *son* had a long life," she replied.

I stepped away, and Helen wiggled the lid back into place, then wheeled the gurney to the gaping maw of the furnace. "Here," I said, "let me give you a hand with that."

"Oh, that's all right," she said. "I do this five or six times a day.

It's not that hard. The gurney has rollers built into the top." She gave a shove to the end of the box, and it slid easily until it was halfway off the gurney and tipped down onto the floor of the furnace. She shoved a little harder, and I heard the bottom of the box scraping along the concrete.

Once the box was all the way in, she removed the cotter pin and pressed the button that lowered the furnace door. She pushed a glowing red button labeled Afterburner, and I heard a low whoosh, like a gas fireplace lighting up. "I knew fighter planes had afterburners," I said. "I didn't know cremation furnaces had 'em, too. Is it faster than the speed of sound?"

She rolled her eyes at the joke.

"Seriously, though, why do you turn on the afterburner first?"

"This is a secondary burner, just before the exhaust flue," she explained. "Makes sure everything's burned before the gases go out the stack. If TVA's power plants burned coal this cleanly, you wouldn't see all that haze between downtown Knoxville and the mountains."

She tapped her finger on a small glass disk set into the door, no bigger than the security peephole in the front door of my house. "You can watch through there if you want," she said, "but you won't be able to see much. Mostly just flame." She reached for a glowing green button labeled Pre-Ignition, and I put one eye to the little window. A jet of yellow flame, roughly the size of the Olympic torch, blossomed from the hole in the roof of the furnace and flickered downward, flaring outward when it hit the lid of the box. Within moments the cardboard began to burn and the flame spread. "Okay," I heard Helen say, "now I'm go- ing to switch on the combustion burner." The bloom of yellow flame suddenly turned blue and filled the entire upper portion of the chamber. I watched, mesmerized, as the cardboard collapsed, revealing the contours of the frail body. And then, for a brief moment before flame and smoke obscured my view altogether, I saw the withered flesh catch fire, and somehow it struck me as a cleansing, even a holy thing. "Ashes to ashes, dust to dust," I heard myself whisper. It was an impromptu benediction from an unlikely source—me, a doubt-filled scientist who dealt daily in death—given to a total stranger, a man I had never seen before, and whom no one would ever see again.

After a moment I stepped back and turned to Helen. She was watching me closely, I noticed, and she seemed slightly embarrassed when I caught her looking. It was as if she knew she'd intruded on some private exchange. "Funny thing," I said. "I see bodies all the time—I actually burned a couple of corpses last week as a research experiment—but this was different. This was a person." She nodded. I could see that she understood what I meant and that I'd eased her embarrassment by what I'd said.

"Do you want to see the 'after' version now?" She pointed at the other furnace, and I stepped four feet to the right. She opened the door, and I felt a blast of heat as the door slid down. A human skeleton was laid out in perfect anatomical order on the concrete floor. The bones were grayish white and brittle-looking, completely calcined. Except for the skull, which had rolled to one side and cracked into several large pieces, and the rib cage, which had caved in like the timbers of a shipwreck, the bones remained intact and in their original positions. "I couldn't have laid it out better myself," I said.

She smiled. "Most people think that when a body's cremated, it comes out of the furnace as cremains," she said. "They have no idea that it's still a recognizable skeleton." She reached in with a gloved hand, pulled out a humerus from the upper arm, and gestured with it. "I always find it fascinating to look at the skeletons," she said. "Every one is different. This one, for example, was a very large woman. About three hundred pounds. I had to really watch the oven temperature on her."

I thought for a moment. "Because of the fat?"

"Right. I learned my lesson on that a long time ago. About six months after I started working here, I had a huge guy come through—he weighed five hundred pounds at least and barely fit in the furnace. This was late one afternoon in December, a few days before Christmas, and it was getting dark around five o'clock. Well, about thirty minutes after I got him going, one of the guys from the place across the street came knocking on the door, asked me if I knew my exhaust stack was red hot. I went out to look, and it was glowing cherry red."

"A five-hundred-pound body's going to have two or three hundred pounds of fat on it," I said. "That's gonna make one heck of a grease fire once it melts and ignites."

"You can say that again," she said. "I came running back in and checked the temperature gauge. Normally these furnaces run at sixteen to eighteen hundred degrees. That guy pushed it up to nearly three thousand. I'm just lucky the roof didn't catch fire. I sure learned my lesson from that."

"So how do you keep that from happening again?"

"The really obese ones, I get 'em going, then throttle the gas back. Once the fat's burning, that pretty much keeps them going for a while. Then, after about forty-five minutes—once I see the temperature drop below sixteen hundred—I relight the combustion burner for another fifteen or twenty minutes. That's enough to bring 'em on home."

"Speaking of obese bodies burning," I said, "you'll be inter-ested in this." There weren't many people I could say something like that to in all seriousness. "We had a master's student a few years ago who did a thesis on spontaneous combustion."

She guffawed. "What did she read for research," she hooted, "the *Weekly World News*?"

"Actually, it was a really good thesis," I said. "One of the best I've ever read. It's not just supermarket tabloid readers who be-lieve in spontaneous combustion. I've talked to several police of-ficers and firefighters who swear they've seen cases of spontane-ous combustion—bodies that were thoroughly incinerated but with very little damage to the surrounding structure, or even the furniture." Helen nodded brightly, and I could tell she was in-trigued. "Anyhow, Angi—the graduate student—found that in all these cases where someone appeared to have burst into flame, the individuals were overweight, and what had occurred was a low-temperature fire. The bodies smoldered for a day or two, without ever burning hot enough to cause the fire to spread."

"So what caused them to burn?"

"Many of them were smokers, so they probably dropped a lit cigarette onto their clothes," I said. "One woman got her sleeve too close to the burner of a gas stove. The combustion wasn't spontaneous; there had to be an ignition source. Alcohol was another common factor—some of them were drunk, others were asleep, so they didn't notice or react fast enough when their clothes or their bed caught fire. They probably died of smoke inhalation pretty quickly, but the fire kept going. As their fat melted, the clothing soaked up the grease, just like the wick of a candle or a lamp."

"You're right," she said, "that *is* interesting."

"But I'm getting you sidetracked," I said. "Show me what you do next."

"It's pretty simple," she said. She lifted a long-handled tool from a pair of brackets attached to the side of the furnace. It was like a cross between a rake and a hoe: welded onto the handle was a wide metal flange, maybe ten inches wide by two inches tall. She maneuvered it through the mouth of the furnace, stretched it all the way to the back—down beyond the woman's feet—and began raking the bones forward. When they reached the front of the furnace, they tumbled down into a wide hopper, which I hadn't noticed until now. She made several passes with the rake-like tool, then switched to a shop broom, with a broad head and stiff bristles. Once she was satisfied she'd swept everything into the hopper, she bent down and removed a square metal bucket from beneath the hopper.

She carried the bucket to a workbench along one wall of the building and tipped out the contents onto a workbench there. Next she grasped a U-shaped handle, which was attached to a block of metal a few inches square. With it she began crushing the bones, almost as if she were making mashed potatoes. After reducing the bones to pieces no more than an inch or two at the biggest, she dragged the block back and forth through the bone fragments. Soon its sides and bottom bristled with industrial-strength metal staples, and I realized it was a magnet.

"Where'd all those staples come from?"

"The bottom of the shipping container," she said. "The sides and top are cardboard, but the bottom is plywood, stapled to the cardboard."

"Makes sense to use plywood," I said. "You don't want the bottom getting soggy and letting the body fall out."

"Exactly," she said. "Most people wouldn't think about that, but you understand because you've seen what happens when bodies start to decompose."

"Doesn't take more than a day or two for fluids to start leaching out," I agreed. "You fish out the staples so they don't go back to the family?"

"That," she said, "and so they don't dull the blades of the processor. I'll show you that in a minute." She stirred around a bit more, snagging a zipper and a few buttons. "Here you go, a Cracker Jack prize," she said. She fished out a short metal bracket drilled with four holes, a scorched screw threaded through each hole. "She must have had a plate in her arm or leg," she said.

"Do you get a lot of orthopedic hardware?"

"More and more, seems like."

"As the Baby Boomers start to die off," I said, "I bet you'll see even more. All those joggers and tennis players and downhill skiers going in for new parts. What do you do with stuff like that?"

"We bury it," she said, "unless the family asks for it."

"So if somebody had a pair of artificial knees and the family wanted them, you'd send 'em back?"

"Absolutely," she said. She took a hand broom and swept the crushed bones into a small mound, then unhooked a large metal dustpan from a peg above the workbench. Bracing the bone fragments with the broom, she slid the dustpan underneath, scooping nearly everything into it with one quick, efficient push. Then she slid it backward about a foot and carefully swept the remaining dust into it.

At the left-hand end of the workbench was a large metal pot, the size and shape of a restaurant kitchen's stockpot. "This is the processor," she said. "You see the blades there in the bottom?" I looked into the vessel and saw a thin, flat bar attached to a bolt at the center. The pot was roughly fifteen inches in diameter; the bar reached about halfway to the sides of the pot. Both ends of the bar had shorter bars attached to what appeared to be bearings or pivots. "If you flip that switch, you'll see how it works." She nodded toward a toggle on the wall just above the container. I flipped it up, and the blades jolted into motion. I caught a brief glimpse of the shorter bars flipping outward toward the rim, and then the whole whirling assembly disappeared, the way an airplane propeller disappears at full throttle. I flipped the switch off, and the blades spun down, the centrifugal force keeping the shorter bars extended until the assembly coasted to a stop.

"That blade assembly looks like what I feel when I jam my hand down into my garbage disposal to untangle the dishrag," I said, giving an involuntary shudder. "You could sure lose a hand in there fast." She nodded again, then tipped the dustpan into the pot. She started an exhaust fan above the processor, then switched on the blades. A plume of dust eddied upward as the blades chewed through the chunks of bone, sending a swirl of powder and small bits of bone up the sides of the vessel. After a half minute or so, she switched off the motor, and the pulverized material settled, the blades sending smaller and smaller waves spinning through the powder as they slowed. She grasped the two handles of the pot, gave a twist to release it from the central shaft that came up from the motor underneath, and hoisted the pot up to the workbench. Then she tipped it into another hopper, this one emptying into a bag of clear, heavy plastic that was cinched to its spout. She tapped the side of the hopper to coax the last bit of powder to fall, then unhooked the bag, dropped in a small metal identification tag, and sealed the bag with a twist tie.

"Where does the tag come from?"

"I make those here," she said. "Each body gets an ID number, which goes in the file and on this tag."

"Just like at the Body Farm," I said. "You've got a good system here."

"Well, I've had twenty years to work out the kinks," she replied, laughing.

The bag was already inside a black plastic container, measuring about six inches by eight inches wide and eight or ten inches tall. She folded down the box's plastic lid and snapped it shut.

"Could I ask one more favor?"

"Sure," she said. "What?"

"Would you mind if I took the bag out and weighed it?"

"Of course not," she said.

Before leaving the Anthropology Department, I'd borrowed the postage scale from Peggy's supply closet. I was curious to see how the cremains I'd received from Burt DeVriess compared in weight to those from the crematorium. Burt's Aunt Jean had weighed barely three pounds. These cremains tipped the scales at nearly twice that. I commented on the difference to Helen. "Well, this gal was pretty good-sized," she said. "Big-boned, as large people like to say."

"It's true," I said. "The heavier you get, the stronger your bones have to be just to carry your body weight. Bones are like muscles—the more you challenge 'em, the stronger they grow."

She smiled. "I like that analogy. Like muscles."

"A little bit longer-lasting, though," I said. "Especially when there's fire involved."

I thanked Helen for the help and headed back to UT. When I got back to the office, I looked again at the cremains Burt

DeVriess had sent me. With the comparison fresh in my mind, I was struck more than ever by how wrong they looked. The bone fragments were too big and splintered. The granular part was too grainy. The powder was too fine. And those pebbles—they were just plain wrong. I'd known it from the moment I saw them; now, somehow, I took them as a personal affront. With the tip of a pencil, I stirred the mixture, frowning, thinking about various tests I could use to determine what precisely was in this urn besides, or instead of, Burt's Aunt Jean.

The phone rang. "Dr. B.?"

"Yes, Peggy?"

"You haven't seen my postage scale, have you?"

Damn—it was on the corner of my desk, where I'd set it and promptly forgotten it upon walking into my office.

"I need to mail Kate Spradley's bound copy of her dissertation to her down in Pensacola, and I can't find the scale to weigh it."

"I'll look around and see if I spy it anywhere," I said.

"Would you like me to pick up one for you next time I'm at Office Depot, Dr. B.?"

"Whatever would I need with a postage scale, Peggy?"

"Heaven only knows," she said. "And I'm pretty sure I don't want to."

When I hung up, I made a mental note to stop by the men's room on my way to her office. If I was lucky, the electric hand dryer would have enough oomph to blow away the coating of human dust from the crematorium.

I wished it could also dispell the layers of dread and fear that had settled over my heart since Garland Hamilton's escape.

# CHAPTER 9

THE PHONE RANG AND I GRABBED FOR IT, HOPING IT was Art—or a reporter, or anyone–calling to tell me Hamilton had been captured.

The caller was Robert Roper, the Knox County district attorney general, but he was calling to ask about Mary Latham. "You're sure she was already dead when the car burned?" Robert was a longtime colleague and friend; I'd testified for him in a dozen or more murder trials over the past decade, and I respected his thoroughness and professionalism. I also appreciated the fact that Robert had recused his entire staff when the police initially charged me with Jess Carter's murder.

"No way she could have been alive," I said. "Not unless she was walking around like somebody out of *Night of the Living Dead,* with hunks of flesh falling off and flies and maggots swarming all over."

"Thanks for sharing," he said. "I was just about to eat lunch. Maybe I'll catch up on my depositions instead."

"If memory serves, you could stand to skip a lunch or two," I parried. "Last time I saw you, you'd put on about twenty pounds."

"You should write a book," he said. "*Dr. Brockton's Gross-Out Weight-Loss Plan.* It could be the next South Beach Diet. You might wind up on *Oprah.*"

"I'll be sure to tell Oprah it was you who inspired me."

"Great. Now back to Mary Latham. Can you tell if she decomposed in the car or someplace else?"

"I doubt it," I said. "Normally there's a big, greasy stain where the decomposition occurred, but the car's interior is probably too badly burned to tell. You might want the crime-scene guys to go back and check the house and the yard—anyplace she might have lain for a couple of days before her husband—or whoever—put her in the car."

"How about the freezer in the basement?"

"Not likely, though it might've been a good idea—if he'd frozen her, she wouldn't have decomposed." I thought for a moment. "Thing is, it would have been messy to get her into the car once she started to decompose. Parts fall off, stuff drips out. It's not easy, and it's sure not pleasant. Of course, if you've resorted to murdering your wife, pleasantness might not be high on your list of priorities at the moment. Still, my guess is she was already in the car. I'd be willing to bet he put her in the passenger seat right after he killed her, drove the car out to that field, and wiggled her over to the driver's seat while she was still fresh. Although he'd be taking a chance on somebody finding her."

"Not much of a chance," said Robert. "That spot's pretty isolated."

"Are you sure it's the husband?"

"Pretty damn sure," he said. "During the three-day period before the car burned, nobody besides the husband seems to have seen her or talked to her."

"Makes sense," I said, "since she was dead."

"There's a big problem with the case against him, though," Roper said.

"What's that?"

"His alibi," he said. "Stuart Latham was in Las Vegas when the car burned. The investigating officer got hold of him on his cell phone, and Latham called back from a landline in the Bellagio Hotel."

"But was he already in Vegas when she was killed? If she'd been dead for days, why does it matter where he was when the car actually caught fire?"

"Because," he said, "a good defense attorney will use that to plant doubt in the minds of the jurors. Make them think somebody else killed her."

"Like who?" I said. "A burglar? Somebody after a stereo or a VCR? Why on earth would some stranger kill her, wait a couple of days, then drive her down to the south forty to burn the evidence? Doesn't create much doubt in my mind."

"You're not a juror," he said, "you're a scientist."

"And anyhow," I persisted, "didn't the husband tell the police she was alive and well when he got on the plane that morning? The decay and the bugs prove he's lying through his teeth."

"You know that, and I know that, but we have to convince twelve other people of that," he said.

"Besides the burned bones, what else was found in the car?"

"Not much," he said. "A few cigarette butts on the ground underneath the driver's window, like maybe she sat there and smoked awhile before the grass caught fire. Husband says she liked to do that. Says he warned her a bunch of times about dropping cigarette butts in the grass. People driving on I-640 saw the smoke and called it in, probably within ten minutes of when it caught fire, according to the arson investigator."

"Any sign of a timer?" I asked. "An ignition device, something he could have set to go off once he was out in Vegas?"

"Not that the evidence techs can find," he said. "One of them's just back from Iraq, and he doesn't see any evidence of an IED."

"What's an IED?"

"Improvised explosive device. Iraqi insurgents use 'em as roadside bombs. They're triggered by a cell phone, sometimes. Thing is, you gotta have some skill with electronics or some training as a terrorist to rig one of those, and Stuart Latham runs an Avis rental-car franchise."

"Well, either he killed her or he didn't," I said in exasperation. "If he did, either he had an accomplice or he didn't. And if he didn't have an accomplice, there ought to be something, either in the car or out at the scene, indicating how he set off the fire from the Bellagio."

"Are you willing to take a look? In the car and out at the property?"

"I'm not an evidence technician," I reminded him.

"But you're great with taphonomy," Roper said. I was impressed the D.A. remembered the term. In archaeology, taphonomy referred to the process or circumstances of fossilization, but forensic anthropologists tended to use it more broadly, to describe the arrangement and relation of bodies, bones, and any other environmental or human-produced evidence that could shed light on a murder or its timing. Postmarked letters, a week-old newspaper open to the sports page, milk or meat tagged with a sell-by date, even a year-old sapling or a seasonal wasp nest within a rib cage or an eye socket—all these could be considered taphonomic evidence of when a murder occurred.

"I'll be glad to take a look at the taphonomy," I said. "Be good for me to get out of the office."

"The car's at the KPD impound lot," he said. "When do you want to see it?"

"How about early in the morning," I said, "while it's a mere ninety degrees?"

"I'll have my investigator, Darren Cash, meet you at the impound lot. Just so you know, we're getting ready to ask a grand jury to indict Stuart Latham for first-degree murder, based on the insect evidence you found in the skull. First, though, we'll get a search warrant to go back for another look at the property. If you find anything else in the car, that could help with the warrant."

"I'll see what I can do," I said, "but don't hold your breath. What time should I meet Cash?"

"How does nine o'clock sound?"

"Sounds late and hot," I said. "What about eight instead?"

"I'll have Darren meet you at eight."

"You mind if Art Bohanan comes along? He wasn't available when the KPD forensics team went over the car."

"I'm always glad to have Art take a look."

AT 7:55 THE NEXT MORNING, Art and I turned onto the lane leading to the KPD impound lot. The lot was on a dead-end street in East Knoxville, directly across I-40 from the zoo. Something about the juxtaposition struck me as funny—hundreds of captive animals on the south side of the interstate, I realized, hundreds of captive vehicles on the north side. As we entered the dead end, I imagined a mass escape from the zoo: animals tunneling under the freeway, then speeding off in stolen cars and trucks—chimpanzees and gorillas driving the getaway vehicles, hippos and elephants hunkering in the back of the biggest trucks. I pointed out a car to Art, a red BMW convertible with the top down. "You think a giraffe could fit into the back of that Beemer?"

Art glanced at me, then at the car, then stared at me as if I were some sort of zoological specimen myself. He raised his eyebrows slowly, then shook his head, an expression of deep pity on his face. "We have *got* to get you some professional help," he said.

"Come on," I said, "it's not that far-fetched. Primates have opposable thumbs—they could hot-wire the ignitions."

"Professional help," he said again. "A mind is a terrible thing to lose."

The impound lot was a quarter mile long—four narrow lots, actually—sandwiched between the interstate on one side and a set of railroad tracks on the other. The first lot, an unfenced pad of gravel about fifty yards square, contained vehicles that would be auctioned off on September 1, a sign announced. These were unclaimed or forfeited cars and trucks, along with several horse trailers, which particularly intrigued me. *Surely I could find a use for a cheap horse trailer at the Body Farm*, I thought.

The second lot was a fenced expanse of asphalt measuring the same fifty yards deep—the depth being dictated by the train tracks bordering the back—but stretching a hundred yards long.

This lot held vehicles that had been towed for a multitude of reasons: Fire hydrants had been blocked, parking meters had gone unfed for weeks on end, junkers had been abandoned alongside the interstate, unpaid traffic tickets had mounted to thousands of dollars. Many of the vehicles had open windows, and several, like the red BMW, were convertibles open to the elements. "Good thing for those convertibles we're in the middle of a drought," I said.

Art shrugged, unconcerned. "If the top's down or the windows are open when we tow it, nothing we can do. We don't have the keys."

I noticed a video camera mounted on a pole at one corner of the lot. "Have you had break-ins, right here in the impound lot?"

"You wouldn't believe what a problem it is," he said. "We had one guy sneak in with wire cutters one night, cut a big hole in the fence, and drive away."

"He hot-wired one of the cars?"

"He had the keys. It was his car."

"He stole his own car from the police?" I couldn't help laughing. "Did y'all catch him?"

Art shook his head. "We got the car back—he ditched it over in North Carolina—but we never got the guy."

"That took some nerve," I said with a touch of admiration.

Next came a lot whose fence was screened by blue tarps. I pointed. "What's in that one?"

"Cars seized from drug dealers, mostly," he said.

"Why the tarps?"

"To keep people from gawking," he said. "Your average drug dealer tends to drive a better class of car—we've got Acuras, Cadillacs, Mercedeses—and we had a problem with looky-loos hanging around window-shopping."

"Seems like the tarps would attract more people," I said. "Make 'em wonder what's in there that you don't want anybody to see."

"There's a troublemaker inside you just waiting to get out," he said.

Art pulled into the fourth lot, which was tucked at the farthest corner of the compound, back behind a security building outfitted with rooftop surveillance cameras at every corner. This lot contained hard-core specimens: cars flattened by high-speed rollovers or accordioned in head-on collisions. Many of them were missing doors and roofs, the metal chewed away by the Jaws of Life or slashed loose with a Sawzall. Several vehicles were covered with tarps—cars in which shootings had occurred, Art said. Off by itself, along the westernmost side of the fence, was the burned-out shell of a car. The windows were gone and the paint had blistered off, but I could tell by the lines that it had been a fairly new and expensive car just a couple of weeks before.

A clean-cut young man in his early thirties was peering into the vehicle's interior. When he heard the crunch of the tires on the gravel, he straightened and turned toward us. He was wearing a short-sleeved blue shirt with a yellow tie. The shirt stretched tight around his neck and shoulders, which looked like they'd been borrowed from an NFL linebacker. His crew cut and military posture suggested he'd been either a soldier or a cop before he became a D.A.'s investigator. As the three of us shook hands all around, I said, "I hear good things about you from your boss."

"You've been talking to my wife?"

I laughed. "No, the district attorney."

"Oh, my day-job boss." He grinned. "I've been lucky so far."

"Lucky my foot," said Art. "Darren was the one who broke the Watkins case last year."

I hadn't been involved in it, but I remembered reading about it and being shocked. "Watkins—that was the guy who took out the two-hundred-thousand-dollar insurance policy on the little girl, then drowned her in the backyard pool?"

Cash nodded. "His granddaughter," he said. "The policy had a two-year waiting period on the death benefit. The really sick thing about that case—"

Art broke in. "You mean besides the fact that a man would drown his own granddaughter?"

"Yeah," said Cash, "even sicker than that. He took out the policy, put in the swimming pool, and then waited exactly twenty-five months. That little girl had a rattlesnake coiled around her feet for two years."

"That is sick," I said. "How on earth could somebody do that to his own granddaughter—for any price, let alone a couple hundred thousand bucks?"

"Some people are just plain evil," Art said. "No other explanation for it, I don't care what the forensic psychologists say."

"I'm inclined to agree with you," I said. "I'm not sure about God anymore, but I'm starting to believe in the devil. Not some red-suited guy with a pitchfork and horns, but regular-looking folks. A guy who drowns his granddaughter in the backyard. A woman who feeds her husband arsenic every night."

"A pedophile who trolls the Internet for gullible kids," said Art.

"A husband who kills his wife," said Cash, "and lets her rot for days before burning her body."

I took that as the investigator's hint that we should get down to business. I nodded toward the burned-out car, a short, sleek

SUV. "This looks like it used to be a pretty nice car," I said. "What is it?"

"Lexus RX, 2006," he said. "Probably around forty thousand new."

"That's a lot," I said. "Would have been cheaper to take her on a hike in the Smokies and push her off a bluff—say she tripped and fell."

"Bill loses more hiking buddies that way," Art said. "Never, ever go to the mountains with him."

Cash laughed. "Thanks for the warning." He nodded at the vehicle. "Book value on the vehicle's more like twenty-five thousand now," he said. "But the bank owns most of that. Deductible on the insurance policy's five hundred. Five hundred is dirt cheap if it works to cover your tracks and give you an alibi."

"Well, it didn't quite do the job," I said, "thanks to the bugs. Let's see if there's anything else to find."

Art and I had brought a few things in the back of my truck. We both unfolded white Tyvek jumpsuits and wriggled into them, looking like overgrown toddlers in baggy sleeper pajamas. I opened the tackle box that held an assortment of tools and took out two sharp-pointed trowels and two pairs of tweezers. I handed one of each to Art, then slid a wire screen out from beneath the tackle box. Each opening in the mesh was four millimeters square—about the size of the end of a set of wooden chopsticks from a Chinese take-out place.

Cash showed me how the body had been found in the car. The woman's legs had been down in the driver's well, her left arm hanging down by her side. Her right arm stretched over near the passenger door. Her torso and head were flopped over to the right also.

"As I understand it," I said, "there were no traces of accelerant found in the interior. Is that right?"

"That's right," Cash said. "Arson dog didn't smell anything, and I'm told that dog has a great nose."

"Sure is thoroughly burned for no accelerant," I said, peering into the burned-out shell of the vehicle. The upholstery was completely gone. The seats had been reduced to charred, rusted springs and support rails. The underside of the roof was fully exposed, the same reddish gray as the vehicle's exterior. The windshields and windows were gone. All that remained of the steering wheel was the steel skeleton, including the empty hub where the airbag had been before it fired.

"Used to be cars had a lot of metal inside," said Art. "Now everything's plastic, and once the car catches fire, that plastic keeps feeding it. It's like pornography."

I stared at him, baffled by the comparison. "Pornography? How so?"

"Hot and nasty," he said. "Temperatures in the passenger compartment can go over two thousand degrees. And all that burning plastic releases all kinds of toxic chemicals. Smoke inhalation can kill you long before the heat does."

I recalled the smoke roiling out of the cars we'd recently burned at the Ag farm—dense black billows seething out the windows and windshields once the glass gave way—and nodded. "Any way to tell where the fire started?"

Cash shook his head. "Not for sure," he said. "The ignition was on, though, so the engine was probably idling. We think either the catalytic converter or the muffler set the grass underneath on fire. Most of these luxury SUVs never get off the pavement, but out in that pasture it'd be easy for the exhaust system to set the grass on fire, especially as hot and dry as it's been. Catalytic converter can get up to nearly a thousand degrees, if the car's fairly new and the converter's still working."

"I bet one of you guys knows the ignition temperature of grass," I said.

"Six hundred degrees," they chorused.

"So if that converter was in contact with the vegetation," I said, "it shouldn't have taken more than a few minutes to start a grass fire."

"Right," said Cash.

"Which begs the question," I said, "if the husband did it, how'd he get fifteen hundred miles away before it started burning?"

None of us had an answer, so Art and I squatted down beside the vehicle—me beside the driver's door, him beside the right rear door—and began sifting through the debris in the floor pan. I didn't find much: A layer of ash. A few bolts, screws, and coins. A couple of phalanges, the smallest bones of the fingers and toes. "Hey," I razzed Art, "how come KPD missed these?"

"Simple," he said. "The car burned late afternoon, right after 'Tiffany' got out of school and got on the Web. I was too busy reading love notes from middle-aged perverts to go out to the Latham farm and look for bones. They had to send the B-team instead."

"We gotta get you off that pedophile assignment," I said.

"I'm training a replacement," he said. "I hope to be back to healthier stuff—gunshots and stabbings and bludgeonings—within a month or so."

Art wasn't finding much more in the back than I'd found in the front: springs, seat-belt buckles, and a few coins down where the rear bench seat once met the seat back—that place where every car accumulates loose change and candy wrappers and stray peanuts. I was about to suggest we call it a morning when I heard Art say, "Hmm. *Hmm.*" From one corner of the backseat, he plucked a tiny scrap of partially burned material. He held it up for Cash and me to inspect. It was charred on the edges, but enough remained for it to be recognizable as a shred of crumpled newspaper, not much bigger than a postage stamp. A few words were still legible: "foreign policy" and "Ira," they read. I mentally supplied the missing *q* on the end of "Iraq."

"Darren," I asked, "any other newspaper found in the vehicle?"

"No."

"This little scrap seems odd, the way it's wedged way down in the corner of the backseat. You expect that with pennies and pens, but not so much with newspaper." I knelt down beside the other corner of the backseat and sifted through the debris. The tip of my trowel teased out another bit, smaller and with no type, from a corner of the page. I recognized the distinctive saw-tooth fringe at the edge of the paper, where the roll of newsprint had been cut with a serrated edge. I craned my neck around to look at Darren. "Was the house searched?"

He nodded.

"I don't suppose you remember whether there was a stack of newspapers?"

"You're right," he said, "I don't remember. Why would newspapers be significant?"

"I'm just thinking out loud," I said. "I remember a case in which a woman had stabbed her husband and decided to burn his body in the house. There were no traces of accelerant, but down behind some of the furniture the arson investigator found wads of newspaper, which she'd used as fuel. A couple more minutes and that paper would have gone up in flames. Luckily, the fire department got the fire out before it reached flashover, so some evidence remained."

"So you're thinking maybe Stuart Latham did the same thing?"

"It's possible," I said. "If there's a stack of papers back at the house with a week's worth missing, that might be a clue that he used newspaper to help goose the fire along."

"We'll see," he said. "We can add that to the search warrant, along with what you and Dr. Garcia told us about the bones and the bugs."

"Maggots never lie," I said. "Unlike husbands."

Art and I bagged the phalanges I'd found in the front floor-board, as well as the two bits of newspaper from the backseat. Art folded and taped the bags shut, then wrote the date and time, along with a brief description of the bones and shreds of paper. Then we pulled off the baggy jumpsuits, which by now were plastered to us with sweat, peeled the gloves off our drip-ping hands, and stuffed the disposable garb into a red biohazard bag, for burning in the morgue's medical-waste incinerator. We gave Cash a sweaty good-bye handshake, then drove back out the way we'd come in—past the drug dealers' cars, past the security building, past the main impound lot and the auction lot.

I pointed at the red convertible again. "That's a pretty small backseat," I said. "The giraffe would probably have to be a baby."

"Not necessarily," said Art. "Not if it was sitting sideways."

# CHAPTER 10

EARLY THE NEXT MORNING, AS THE SUN STRUGGLED
to burn through a layer of steamy haze, I threaded my way out
of Sequoyah Hills and along Kingston Pike. Instead of taking the right onto Neyland and along the river to the stadium,
I turned left onto Concord. I bumped across the railroad crossing, then took a right onto Sutherland Avenue, over another set
of tracks and past the dusty silos of a pair of concrete plants,
Sequatchie Concrete and Southern Precast, their gravel parking
lots filled with powdered cement trucks, highway culverts, and
staircases. Next, through the pillars of the Alcoa Highway via-
duct, I glimpsed the white storage tanks of the Rohm and Haas
plastics factory. One of the tanks carried a cartoonish painting
of a bespectacled scientist in a white lab coat, captioned *That's
Good Chemistry*. As I wrinkled my nose against the acrid fumes
of superglue, or one of its chemical cousins, I thought, *More like
"That's Stinky Chemistry."* Then I laughed out loud at the iro-

ny of me, the founder of the Body Farm, complaining about any other establishment's unpleasant smell.

I well knew superglue's affinity for human fingers and finger-prints—I'd glued my fingers together on more than one occa-sion, and Art had actually patented a superglue-fuming device, "the Bohanan Apparatus," used by crime labs nationwide to pick up latent prints on guns, knives, paper, even victims' skin. As I sniffed my way past Rohm and Haas, I imagined every square inch of the factory and its workers to be covered with hand-prints—layer upon layer of loops and whorls, captured forever in superglue fumes and drifting concrete dust.

Middlebrook Pike was the next intersection after I passed Rohm and Haas. I turned left on Middlebrook, heading west, away from downtown. The road burrowed beneath I-40 and then, an industrialized mile later, crossed over the I-640 bypass. Just beyond 640 the cityscape gave way to farmland, and I knew I'd reached the Latham property. The entire Middlebrook front-age, perhaps half a mile, was lined with white board fence. Huge oaks and tulip poplars dotted rolling meadows, and a small stream—Third Creek, if I remembered Knoxville's prosaic creek-naming scheme correctly—meandered out of the property beside an entry road.

The driveway led to a two-story white clapboard farmhouse, easily a century old, shaded by more of the towering oaks. The house was simple but graceful, with a wide, airy porch and gener-ous windows of wavy antique glass. A handful of law-enforcement vehicles, including a crime-lab van, lined a semicircular drive that approached the front porch. Off to the side of the house was a yellow Nissan Pathfinder, which I guessed to be Stuart Latham's.

Beyond the house, after the asphalt drive gave way to gravel, stood a large whitewashed barn, complete with weather vane and lightning rods atop the metal roof. I'd passed this property many times, but I'd never realized how big it was, or how beautiful. Beyond the barn a dirt track led farther out, winding into the pasture, where a pond glistened in a low hollow. The dirt track looped down past the pond, then angled up a hillside beyond. The only jarring notes in the whole pastoral, picturesque scene, a mere two miles from the heart of downtown Knoxville, were the black circle of grass and the blue strobes of the unmarked car belonging to Darren Cash, who'd told me where to meet him.

Cranking down my window—the morning was already hot but not yet unbearable—I caught the sweet, dusty fragrance of hay, a welcome change from the chemical fumes that had forced their way into my truck only a few minutes before. I idled past the barn, around the pond, and up the rise toward Cash, taking my time so I could enjoy the view. Cash was half sitting, half leaning on the trunk of his car, his arms folded, his biceps stretching the limits of a navy polo shirt. As I pulled alongside and parked, just outside the scorched circle, Cash used one foot to shove off from the rear wheel, then extended his hand through my open window for me to shake. Now that my engine was off, I could hear the steady whoosh of traffic somewhere through the woods to the north—not loud but surprising, considering I could see no signs of the bypass from here.

"Morning, Doc," Cash said. "Nice place, huh?"

"Very nice," I agreed, clambering out. "I wouldn't mind having a place like this myself."

"Well, it could be coming on the market soon," he said. "If we're smart or lucky."

"How long you been here?"

"About an hour. We were waiting for Latham at the gate down at the bottom of the driveway when he headed for work. He wasn't too happy to see our little caravan."

"Did he go on to work?"

"No way," said Cash. "He's in the house, acting all indignant, watching the evidence techs like a hawk. Trying to figure out what they're looking for."

I studied the burned circle, which measured maybe twenty yards across, then turned and looked back toward the house, which was barely visible. "For a place that's as close to downtown as my house, this is mighty isolated," I said. "I can see why nobody would have just happened by and seen a body in the car."

He nodded. "Latham says she liked to park up here when she wanted to think. Sit and smoke and look at the view."

I gazed out over the farmland. From the rise where we stood, the pasture had lovely views to both the east and the west. "Actually, I'll buy that part of the story," I said. "I'd probably do the same if I owned this chunk of land. Except for the smoking."

"Which Latham mentioned three times in his statement. He actually said, 'It was probably a cigarette butt that caught the grass on fire.' When I read his statement the other day, I could almost feel his elbow nudging me in the ribs every time he mentioned the smoking."

"That's because he thinks cops are dumb," I said. "Wanted to make sure they got it."

"Another interesting thing about this location," said Cash. "Once the car was burning, hundreds of people would have seen the smoke from 640—it's only a quarter mile through those trees. Half a dozen people called 911 to report a fire—which I'm sure he wanted."

"To establish the time of the fire," I said.

"Exactly. The first call came at three fifty-three p.m.—while he was playing the slots in the Bellagio."

Cash led me into the burned circle, pointing out four evidence flags, which indicated where the corners of the vehicle had been. A fifth flag marked the spot where five cigarette butts—almost but not quite consumed by the blaze—had been found below the driver's door. I knelt and inspected that area, seeing nothing but the charred stubble of grass and the thin wire of the evidence flag jammed into the ground.

I pointed back toward where the rear of the vehicle would have been. "Do you remember which side the exhaust pipe was on?"

"The right," he said.

Staying well clear of the imaginary vehicle's boundaries, I walked back to what would have been the vehicle's right rear corner and knelt again. The grass there looked exactly like the grass everywhere else within the circle of burned vegetation. "Any idea where the catalytic converter on a Lexus RX is?"

He shrugged. "Um . . . somewhere between the engine and the end of the tailpipe?"

"No wonder your boss thinks so highly of you," I said. "Every answer at your fingertips. Just like on *CSI*." I dropped to my hands and knees and crawled forward, toward what would have been the center of the vehicle, scanning from side to side as I crept. I wasn't sure what I was looking for, and I wasn't sure what it was when I found it. But it was something.

Cash came to the edge of the rectangle and squatted down, but he couldn't see anything from there.

"I've got a big pair of tweezers in the tackle box in my truck," I said. "You mind going and getting it?"

He didn't answer; he just headed to the truck. He might not know a lot about vehicle exhaust systems, but he was easygoing and he didn't seem overly impressed with his own importance. When he handed me the tweezers, I maneuvered the tips down through the burned stalks of grass, squeezed gently, and plucked out the small black shape that had caught my eye. It was hard, oval—more or less—and pinched in the center. Looking closely, I saw that the pinch in the center was caused by a bit of heavy wire, clamped tight.

I held it out for Cash's inspection. "Any idea what that is?"

"None," he said.

"You think it could be something off the underside of the car? A hose clamp or fuel-line fitting or some such?"

He shrugged once more. "You're asking the guy who had no idea where the catalytic converter would be?"

"You're right." I laughed. "What was I thinking?"

"We could check with the mechanics at the Lexus dealership," he said. "Maybe one of those guys would recognize it."

"See, you come up with a good idea every now and then," I said.

He grinned. "Even a blind squirrel finds some nuts."

Something about the shape was familiar to me. Not the blackened blob but the heavy wire. I couldn't place it, though, and when Cash held out an evidence bag, I deposited my find inside. Cash sealed and dated it, but then his pen hesitated.

"Problem?"

"We have to list everything we confiscate when we return the warrant to the judge," he said. "I've got no idea what to call this."

"Call it 'blackened blob,'" I suggested helpfully.

He shot me an unamused look.

"Or 'unidentified burned object recovered from beneath area of burned car.'"

"That sounds better," he said. "I can see why they think highly of you at UT."

Cash and I both went over the rest of the area beneath and surrounding the car, but neither of us found anything else, so he headed back to the house and I headed for UT. As I'd done on my way in, I drove slowly to savor the view. Just as I was nearing the barn, my peripheral vision snagged on something. I stopped the truck and backed up. About ten feet to the left of the dirt track was a small, neat oval, about one foot by two feet, sketched by scorched earth and burned grass. I got out and knelt, using the tip of a pen to sift through the charred stalks. I found nothing. All the same, I retrieved two evidence flags from the back of my truck. I stuck one right beside the circle and the other ten feet away, at the nearest edge of the dirt track.

As I turned from the driveway onto Middlebrook Pike toward downtown, I phoned Cash on his cell, describing what I'd seen and where to find the markers. "Maybe it's nothing," I said.

"Maybe," he said. "But maybe not."

"Maybe a blind squirrel just found a nut," I said.

# CHAPTER 11

**I BOUNDED INTO THE BONE LAB JUST BEFORE LUNCH-**
time, eager to tell Miranda about my finds at the Latham farm.
She wasn't there.

Normally, unless she was out helping me recover a body or
bones from a death scene or dashing to the Body Farm to deliver
a corpse or retrieve a skeleton, Miranda practically lived in the
osteology lab. I could count on walking in to find her bent over
a lab table, measuring bones and keying the dimensions into the
Forensic Data Bank. Every skeleton we got—and this year we'd
get nearly 150, arriving at the Farm as fully fleshed cadavers and
departing bare-boned—had to be measured, their dozens of dimensions added to the data bank. The work was tedious and
time-consuming, and most of it was done by Miranda. Perhaps
I should have been happy she was getting a brief break, but instead I felt slightly annoyed that she wasn't here to listen.

I glanced at Miranda's computer screen—the scene of so much

Googling—and noticed a map filling the display. It was a street map of Knoxville's North Hills neighborhood, which happened to be Miranda's neighborhood. It struck me as odd that Miranda would need a map of her own neighborhood.

I picked up the phone on the desk and dialed Peggy, one floor up. "Have you seen Miranda this morning?"

"She left about fifteen minutes ago," said Peggy. "Said she was going over to the morgue to use the dissecting microscope there."

"The dissecting 'scope? What for?"

"I didn't ask and she didn't tell," said Peggy. "Just like the military's policy on gays."

"Great," I said, "because hasn't *that* approach worked well."

Peggy's mention of the morgue made me want to tell Garcia about my visit to the Latham farm, too, so instead of dialing the morgue and asking for Miranda or him, I hopped into my truck and dashed across the river to the rear of the hospital. Parking in the no-parking zone by the morgue's loading dock, I punched the code to open the door, crossed the garagelike intake area, and threaded my way down the hall to the microscopy lab. The anthropology department had one dissecting 'scope—a stereoscopic microscope, with a micrometer-adjustable stage—but there was sometimes heavy competition for it, so I could understand why Miranda might have come over to use one of the three here at the morgue. She wasn't in the lab, although I did see her backpack, sitting on a table beside one of the 'scopes. A small, U-shaped bone rested on the stage—a hyoid bone, from a throat—and I guessed Miranda was inspecting it for fractures, possible evidence of strangulation. I flipped on the microscope's lamp and took a quick look myself. The arc of bone was smooth and unbroken, except by the tiny numerals "49-06," inked on the bone in Miranda's neat hand, signifying that the hyoid was from the forty-ninth body back in 2006. Number 49-06 had clearly not been strangled, which was both unsurprising and also somewhat reassuring, since this particular man's body had been donated, if memory served, by his widow.

Figuring maybe Miranda had gone to the restroom, I went down the hall to Edelberto Garcia's office to tell him the latest from the Latham case. His door was half open, so I knocked and leaned my head in.

Garcia was standing behind his desk, Miranda leaning over from the other side. On the desk between them, in a circle of light cast by a lamp, was a piece of paper. Miranda's index finger was tracing a zigzag on the page, which I recognized as a map—the same map I'd seen on her computer monitor. When I walked in, she straightened and removed her hand from the map. She looked embarrassed, and for some reason that made me feel embarrassed, too.

"Oh, excuse me," I said awkwardly. "I didn't mean to interrupt."

"Hello, Bill," said Garcia, making my name rhyme with "wheel." "Come in. You're not interrupting."

But I *was* interrupting, I knew; I just couldn't tell exactly *what* I was interrupting. "I was on my way to the research facility," I said to him, "and I wanted to tell you a couple of new things about the Latham case."

"Yes, please," he said. "What is it?"

I told him about going out to the impound lot with Art and Darren Cash, and finding the bits of newspaper in the backseat. I also told him about my trip to the farm, and about finding the wire-cinched blob of material and the small oval of burned grass.

"That's very interesting," he said. But he didn't seem as interested as I'd hoped he would. And I no longer felt as interested as I'd been when I bounded into the bone lab. I'd wanted to ask Miranda what she made of all of this, since she knew Stuart Latham, but this didn't seem the right time or place. A silence hung in the air.

Finally Garcia said, "Was there anything else, Bill?"

"No," I said, looking from his face to Miranda's, then back again. "That was it. I'll see you later." I withdrew, then leaned partway back in. "Did you want this open or closed?" I heard something in my voice—an undertone of suspicion or hurt feelings—that I didn't much like. I hoped neither of them heard it.

"Oh, open of course," said Garcia smoothly.

I turned and retraced my steps down the hall, past the microscope lab, where Miranda's open backpack still sat. It hadn't moved, but it had changed—the map she was sharing with him had been printed in the bone lab, I felt sure, and brought to Garcia in the backpack. I drove back to the stadium feeling suddenly guilty and afraid. Afraid of what? I couldn't have said, but a series of faces flashed in my mind's eye: Miranda's. Jess's. Garland Hamilton's. Stuart Latham's. Edelberto Garcia's. The faces of women I cared for—and men who threatened them, in reality or in my overactive imagination.